The Scottish Thistle Amulet: Blessing or Curse?

The Scottish Thistle Amulet: Blessing or Curse?

DANGEROUS DECEPTIONS

LYNNE SMYLES

ILLUSTRATED BY CAROL SCHULTE

THE SCOTTISH THISTLE AMULET: BLESSING OR CURSE?
DANGEROUS DECEPTIONS

iUniverse books may be ordered through booksellers or by contacting:

iUniverse
1663 Liberty Drive
Bloomington, IN 47403
www.iuniverse.com
844-349-9409

ISBN: 978-1-6632-6654-5 (sc)
ISBN: 978-1-6632-6655-2 (e)

Library of Congress Control Number: 2024920905

Print information available on the last page.

iUniverse rev. date: 10/21/2024

Acknowledgments

I'd like to express my heartfelt appreciation to Dianne Bogdan, editor extraordinaire, for her dedication and expertise in editing *The Scottish Thistle Amulet.* Dianne's probing questions and insightful suggestions have always had a positive influence on my writing. Upon completing a chapter, I would ask myself, *WWDD?* (What would Dianne do?) This question would cause me to reflect on my writing and would inevitably send me back to the drawing board. Thank you, dear friend, for your guidance and encouragement.

A special thank-you to my extremely talented niece Terri Lyn Hermann for her astute observations and recommendations regarding elements of the story. Her creative suggestions added an additional layer of intricacy to the Scottish thistle theme with her unique ability to pique the reader's curiosity. I'm exceedingly fortunate for Terri Lyn, an accomplished writer herself, for offering her time and acumen.

The elaborate detailed illustrations created by Carol Schulte, illustrator and cherished friend, complement and enhance the story's narrative. Each illustration sent for my approval was like opening a present on Christmas morning. The anticipation was exhilarating. Every illustration is a beautiful rendition, capturing the essence of the narration. Thank you, Carol, for the numerous hours spent on creating extraordinary artwork for our readers to enjoy.

A special thank-you to my husband, David Smyles. His love and support continue to be an inspiration.

And many thanks to my readers. Your continued support is the impetus that inspires me to keep writing. Riley and Charlie are eager for you to join them on their trip to Scotland. Will this turn out to be an ordinary vacation for the cousins, or … Well, you'll just have to wait and read.

Thank you, Remy Convery, for the five-star review on my previous book, *The Haunting of Whispering Cove Lighthouse*, posted on the Goodreads website. I appreciate the insightful critique of the book. I would also like to thank you for suggesting that Goodreads include my book on their site.

He was almost giddy with the anticipation of getting his hands on the priceless Scottish Thistle antiquity.

Prologue

Edinburgh, Scotland, 1932

Lars Eriksson envisioned himself as a man of opportunity. Although he was a skilled tradesman, he preferred to use his intellect to devise intricate schemes to swindle unsuspecting people out of their valuable possessions.

And now as he inched his way through the dark, narrow tunnel that snaked its way beneath the Museum of Edinburgh, he fingered the Thor's hammer necklace dangling from the chain around his neck. He wore it for the Norwegian god's strength. Tonight, he would prove the necklace's worth! As he continued his trek, a smile came across his face as he reflected on the translation of his name: Lars meaning "success in life," and Eriksson meaning "eternal ruler." In Lars's eyes, both names seemed to define the man he had become.

Beads of perspiration formed on his forehead and upper lip. A cold trickle of sweat ran down the small of his back, causing a slight chill. This was it! After months of preparation, his plan was about to come to fruition. He was almost giddy with the anticipation of getting his hands on the priceless Scottish thistle antiquity. He couldn't recall how many times he had gazed upon the exquisite thistle amulet as he passed it on his way to his refurbishing job in the far wing of the museum. As a young boy living in Norway, he had heard stories of the renowned artifact and its history.

Although the descriptions were vivid, words couldn't begin to describe its beauty. The amulet's thistle was designed with flawlessly cut amethyst stones that, when struck by the light, sent out an explosion of dancing purple shards against the mirrored display case. The thistle's bud and stem were composed of dazzling kelly-green emeralds. The opulent jeweled thistle was embedded in an ornate polished silver oval setting.

This next caper would be the crown jewel of his career.

The artifact had been donated to the museum by the royal family in recognition of the brave Scottish soldiers who had defeated the Norsemen at Ayrshire. It was the Museum of Edinburgh's most valued possession.

Although the thistle's value was Lars's top priority, it wasn't the only driving force behind his obsession to obtain the relic. It was its legendary history, a thorn in his side. He recalled the story that had been handed down from father to son about how the thorn had saved the lives of the Scottish soldiers after the Norse king had sent longships to Largs in Ayrshire in

1263 to ambush the Scottish soldiers as they slept, kill them, and take over the land. Supposedly, the Norsemen removed their shoes in order to take the Scottish soldiers by surprise. Because of being shoeless, one of the Norseman had stepped on a thistle and yelled out in agonizing pain. That cry alerted the Scottish soldiers, rousing them and thereby enabling them to defeat their attackers and save the homeland. So, to the people of Scotland, the thistle was and is a symbol of bravery, strength, and determination. But to Lars, the thistle represented a nocuous weed that inadvertently contributed to the demise of the Norwegian soldiers.

As he emerged from the secret tunnel, which he had fortuitously discovered while repairing a wall, Lars could see the opportunity of a lifetime just a few feet away. He moved ahead cautiously, listening for any signs of an intruder. With smooth, precise movements, he extracted the amulet, careful to avoid setting off any alarms. With those same precise movements, he turned and was back moving through the tunnel and heading for the vehicle that would provide his escape to St. Andrews.

The drive to St. Andrews took a little more than an hour. At this time of night there were few cars on the road, so Lars was able to cruise along at a comfortable speed even in his rattletrap of a car. Occasionally he would glance in the rearview mirror just to make sure that he wasn't being followed.

This little trinket will set me up for the better part of my life, he thought as he touched the velvet-wrapped amulet stashed in his coat pocket. He already had a buyer in Norway who was anxious to get his hands on the amulet.

Finally reaching his destination, Lars pulled onto a secluded road that ran along the water. Too excited to sleep, he decided to stretch his legs and climb to the top of a rocky sandstone cliff to get a better view of the turbulent sea below. He felt exhilarated as he breathed in the chilly night air. His fixation on the amulet prompted him to pull the treasure from his pocket. Just one more look before he hid it away for safekeeping.

Lars unwrapped the antiquity from its velvet covering. It was extraordinary! Even in the dark, its facets seemed to catch the moonbeams, creating sparks of purple and green. Lars wrapped the amulet back in its protective cloth. He was just about to return it to his pocket when a noise startled him. He pivoted quickly in the direction of the sound. The abrupt movement caused him to lose his footing.

In Lars's effort to catch himself, the amulet flew from his hand and landed in an old archaeological dig at the foot of the cliffs. An avalanche of rock and debris cascaded down the side of the cliff, burying the treasure. Grasping at a jagged outcrop of rock, Lars finally regained his balance. As he was about to head down the cliff to look for the relic, another huge chunk of sandstone broke off. This time Lars wasn't so lucky.

As he began to fall, he felt a sudden yank. A branch jutting out from a tree tenaciously rooted in the sandstone caught the Thor necklace he was wearing, ripping it from his neck. The last image seared into his brain was that of the priceless antiquity. His final thought before his body hit the rocks far below was of how this cursed, wretched weed not only had caused the death of the brave Norwegian soldiers but also was responsible for his own demise.

"It's cursed!" he howled, his cry sounding like that of a wounded animal. Then came silence. The only sound was the tumultuous sea, which seemed to have swallowed up Lars's angry whine along with his broken, crumpled body.

Chapter One

From Marine City, Michigan—Scotland, Here We Come!

"Hello, Aunt Eleanor? Riley? Anybody home?" Charlie called though the screen door.

"We're in the living room," his aunt answered. Charlie walked into the room to find his aunt and Riley poring over some paperwork.

"Hey, Aunt Eleanor. How are your roots coming along?" he asked as he sat down. Eleanor's hand automatically went to her hair, her brow creasing with a look of concern. Charlie quickly realized his poor choice of words.

"No. No. Not your hair roots. I meant your ancestry. I thought that you were going to explore your heritage like Uncle Donald did."

"Oh. OK, Charlie, you're forgiven," his aunt replied with a self-conscious laugh. "I've shelved that project for a while. Your uncle has just received some extraordinary news. He's been awarded a contract to redesign a portion of St. Andrew's College in Scotland. The contractors want him there in a couple of weeks to go over the plans. I was just reviewing the itinerary with Riley when you popped in." She handed him the paperwork. "Linda and Greg McGregor, associates of your uncle, own a house in St. Andrews, and they've offered to let us stay there during the construction. They also mentioned that they have a niece and nephew, Grant and Kenzie McGregor, living in St. Andrews. They're twins, and both have qualified through their high school science department to take an introductory class in archaeology at the University of St. Andrews this summer. Linda gave them our phone number thinking that it may be fun for you to meet up. They can show you around the school and town."

"That's a wonderful idea," Riley agreed. "I bet they know about sights that most tourist don't get to see."

"Oh, so you're going to be gone for the rest of the summer," Charlie said, handing the papers back, looking a bit crestfallen. "It sounds like a great trip. I've seen some pictures of the buildings in St. Andrews. They look like something out of a *Harry Potter* movie. You're going to get some great shots with that new camera of yours, Riley. I'm looking forward to seeing them when you get home."

"How about seeing them in person?" Riley asked, already knowing what her cousin's response would be. "Your parents have already agreed to the trip."

"I'm in! I can see it now: the dynamic duo hits Scotland, where mysteries and legends are lurking around every corner. Hey! Maybe we'll solve the mystery of the Loch Ness Monster." Charlie laughed as he gave his cousin a high five. Riley just shook her head and rolled her eyes. *Sometimes Charlie can be such a dork,* she thought.

Riley and Charlie filled the next couple of weeks with enjoyable activities with their friends Margaret and Tom Warner, a brother and sister who spent the summer at a cottage down the canal. A favorite outing was biking into town for some ice cream from the Sweet Tooth Shop. When Tom was off fishing, Margaret and Riley would buzz up to MC Marketplace to check out the latest summer arrivals. Other days were spent inventing different ways to surf behind the speedboat, for example, nailing a chair to the surfboard so one could sit or stand on the chair while surfing. And there was always that take-your-life-in-your-hands sail on *Bree-Z*, Riley's Sunfish. Sailing with Riley—well, anyone who had ever sailed with her would attest that it wasn't for the faint of heart.

Although Riley and Charlie loved hanging out with their friends, they were eager for the upcoming trip to Scotland. And now they were finally boarding the plane—wheels up! Had Riley and Charlie known what lay ahead of them in St. Andrews, perhaps they would have remained in Marine City, a much safer place to spend the rest of their summer.

Chapter Two

The Million-Dollar Question

Eight hours later, the plane touched down in England. From there the family caught a connecting flight to Edinburgh, a city in Scotland. After deplaning, retrieving their luggage, and renting a car, they were off to do some sightseeing. Their first stop was Edinburgh Castle. Because they were on a tight schedule, their tour had to be limited if they were going to complete all the things on their to-do list. A double-decker bus ride was a unique way for the family to glean a bit of interesting history of the town.

The last stop was the Museum of Edinburgh. After an hour in the museum, the group was about to leave when they came across an unusual showcase. Instead of displaying the actual artifact, there was a picture of an amulet titled "Scottish Thistle." Written below the picture was an inscription that read, "Donated by the royal family in commemoration of our brave Scottish soldiers."

"Why wouldn't they display the actual piece of jewelry instead of a picture?" Riley asked her parents. The curator of the museum was standing close by and heard Riley's question.

"Excuse me," she said as she approached the family. Riley turned to face the speaker. The curator was an attractive woman in her late thirties.

"Hello, my name is Barbara Macpherson. I'm the curator here at the museum. I think that I can answer your question about the missing artifact. Always happy to help our visitors from across the pond!"

"Hi, nice to meet you," Riley replied. She introduced herself and the rest of the family to the curator.

"Is there a mystery involved in the missing treasure?" Charlie inquired with raised eyebrows and a tinge of excitement in his voice.

"I'm going to let you decide after you hear the story," the curator said with a subtle smile. She could tell by the looks on Riley's and Charlie's faces that the two hoped the details of the tale would lead to a secret riddle that was itching to be solved.

"The Scottish thistle amulet went missing in 1932. During that time, the museum was undergoing renovation in the far west wing of the building. The authorities believe that a worker by the name of Lars Eriksson, who had been working on the renovation, snuck in through an underground tunnel, stole the amulet, and made his way to St. Andrews."

"Why was he a suspect?" Riley asked, hungry for more information.

"Well, he was the only carpenter who failed to show up for work when the museum reopened the following week."

"OK, but how did the police know that he went to St. Andrews?" Charlie inquired. "Did he leave some kind of clue behind?"

"No, sorry to say. The gruesome reality is that a body washed ashore several weeks later. That body was identified as belonging to Lars Eriksson. So, the police concluded that Lars had taken the amulet and was planning to leave St. Andrews by boat when something led to his death. They don't believe his death was due to drowning because of the several broken bones discovered during the autopsy. It was determined that his death was likely caused by a fall, possibly from a nearby cliff," Macpherson finished with a pained expression on her face.

"What do they think happened to the amulet?" Dad asked, his curiosity now piqued.

"No one knows," Ms. Macpherson responded with a shrug. "It might have gotten lost at sea. It might have fallen from Lars's pocket, if in fact he did climb up the cliff. Or he might have hidden it somewhere nearby until he was ready to leave the country. All that I can say is that it has been and always will remain a mystery.

"Oh! There's the director; he's signaling for me to come over. It's been very nice chatting with you. If you have any questions about the origin of the amulet, you can email me at this address," she said, handing Riley her card. As Ms. Macpherson turned to walk away, she stopped to pick up a pamphlet lying on the floor next to the exhibit. As she knelt down to retrieve the paper, she couldn't help but overhear the exchange between the teens and Riley's parents.

"Can you believe that the missing treasure could be in the same town where we're staying?" Charlie whispered to his cousin, as the family turned to leave.

"When we get to the house, the first thing that we are going to do is to research cliffs in the area," Riley replied with a conspiratorial smile.

"Oh yeah!" Charlie said, giving his cousin a low five.

"All right, you two, no more chasing mysterious treasure," Mom scolded. "Have you already forgotten the trouble, let alone the danger, of your last escapade? In your overzealous pursuit of Captain Boyle's pirate treasure, you nearly drowned when the boat drifted away. If that wasn't dangerous enough, you were kidnapped and almost thrown overboard. I would think that's enough excitement for a lifetime!"

"Your mom's right. Let's just enjoy Scotland like regular tourists. I'm sure there'll be enough to keep you two busy when you meet the twins," Dad added.

Sounds like the family's staying in St. Andrews for their vacation, Ms. Macpherson thought. *I just bet those two don't heed Riley's parents' advice. It sure would be ironic if two teenagers solved a mystery that the authorities have failed to unravel. You never know, with a fresh pair of eyes and a new perspective, they just might uncover something.* Ms. Macpherson followed the director out of the hall.

The director wanted to speak to Macpherson about overseeing and cataloguing the next three months' shipments of antiquities being delivered to the St. Andrews Museum, a Victorian mansion located in Kinburn Park. The curator of the museum had left suddenly, leaving the museum director in dire need of Barbara's help. He explained that she would be expected to arrive at the museum by the end of the week, if that would work for her. Barbara was flattered and reassured the director that it wouldn't be a problem.

Hmm, who knows, maybe I might run into those two rogue detectives while I'm in town, she thought, chuckling about the possibility.

Chapter Three

Fellow Conspirators

The family arrived at Kirkland Cottage late that evening. There was still enough light to see the quaint beauty of the residence. The entryway had a stone-walled front yard equipped with a firepit, a barbecue grill, and a patio table and chairs.

"This is lovely," Mom exclaimed, setting her suitcases down as she waited for Dad to unlock the front door. The floor plan was perfect for accommodating the foursome. The ground floor's spacious open plan consisted of a kitchen and a living/dining room with a wood-burning stove. Down the hall was the master bedroom with an attached master bath. Upstairs were two bedrooms with a bathroom at the end of the hall. After their quick tour, the group went to their rooms, unpacked, and met back in the living area for a bite to eat. Linda had seen to it that the caretaker had stocked the refrigerator with enough essentials for the next couple of days, until the family was able to go grocery shopping.

"Ah, not to complain, but did anyone ask about Wi-Fi?" Charlie inquired, looking around the room.

"Sorry, guys, but I don't think the cottage is set up for the internet," Dad replied. "Looks like we'll have to use the internet service at one of the cafes, or I'm sure they have service at the college. Anyway, I'm beat. Time to turn in. I've got a big day tomorrow." He headed for the bedroom.

"Right behind you, Dad," Riley said, getting up from the couch.

"Yeah, Riley and I have a big day ahead too," Charlie replied with a devilish look on his face. Charlie's expression didn't go unnoticed by his aunt Eleanor.

"Just what sort of big day do the two of you have planned?" Mom asked, her voice clearly showing her disapproval.

"I mean, well, don't you remember that we're supposed to meet Grant and Kinsey tomorrow? You know, that kind of big day," Charlie answered, hoping to sound convincing.

"Right. Good night, you two. See you in the morning," Mom said, shaking her head.

"Hey, Riley, what do you think Grant and Kenzie will be like? Do you think that they'll be into solving mysteries? Maybe they can tell us more about the amulet," Charlie whispered.

"I don't have a clue, Charlie. We'll just have to wait and see. If they're both interested in archaeology, it must mean that they're curious about the past. Isn't it all about finding clues and piecing them together to find answers? Fingers crossed that they're up for some investigating. Sightseeing will be great, but now that we know about the missing amulet, it'll be hard to concentrate on anything else," Riley admitted.

Kenzie called early the following morning to see if she and Grant could stop by and meet the family on their way to the college. Riley and Charlie were dressed and ready when the two arrived at the cottage.

One would never have guessed that Grant and Kenzie were twins. Grant was about six feet tall with tan skin and an athletic build. His jet-black hair was the perfect frame for his mischievous, penetrating blue eyes. His roguish, infectious smile caused people to like him immediately. Kenzie, on the other hand, was around five foot five with blonde hair that was loosely caught up in a long messy braid at the nape of her neck. The only similarities to Grant were her tanned athletic frame and her blue eyes. However, unlike her brother, Kenzie's eyes were more contemplative.

After introductions were made and pleasantries were exchanged, the twins arranged to meet Riley and Charlie at St. Rule's Tower later that morning to do some sightseeing.

"What's on your agenda, Mom?" Riley asked as she helped tidy up the kitchen.

"I'm going to catch the bus to St. Andrews Botanic Garden and do some sketching," Mom answered as she began gathering her art supplies. "The garden is known for its wide variety of flowers, wildlife, rock gardens, and Tangled Bank, a new attraction with sand dunes, meadows, and glades."

"Well, Aunt Eleanor, with all those opportunities for sketches, we might not see you again until it's time to go back to the States." Charlie laughed as he held the door open for his aunt. Dad followed Mom outside.

"See you two for dinner. We'll probably eat around six," Mom called back over her shoulder. "And try to remember that you're meeting Grant and Kinsey to go sightseeing. There had better be no sleuthing schemes up your sleeves!"

Riley held up her camera and gave her mom a thumbs-up. An hour later, Riley and Charlie were on their way to meet their friends. They arrived at St. Rule's Tower early. Looking up, the teens guessed that the structure was taller than one hundred feet. The gray sandstone exterior gave it a medieval appearance.

"Are you up for a climb?" Charlie challenged his cousin, looking up at the stone structure.

"Do they allow tourists up there?" Riley asked, searching for information on the tower.

"They must," replied Charlie. "When I was checking out the building, I thought that I saw a woman wearing a white dress passing by the window."

"Are you sure that you saw someone in the window?" she asked her cousin.

"Well then, Cousin, you're on!" Riley said, accepting the dare. The two entered the structure and made their way to the top of the extremely narrow metal spiral stone staircase with one hundred fifty-six steps. The view was breathtaking. Riley began taking pictures of the St. Andrews Cathedral ruins, the harbor, the countryside, and the charming, picturesque town of St. Andrews. After capturing the spectacular scenery with her camera, Riley looked around the empty room.

"Are you sure that you saw someone in the window?" she asked her cousin. "Because there's no one here now. She must have just—*poof!*—vanished into thin air."

"I'm sure that I did. It was just a glimpse, but I swear that she was there. Maybe there's a different way to exit," Charlie suggested. "We'd better get going if we're going to meet Grant and Kenzie on time." The two got down to the street just in time to greet their friends.

"So, you climbed St. Rule's Tower. What did you think?" Grant asked, smiling, as he approached Riley and Charlie.

"It was incredible!" Riley exclaimed. "I got some fantastic shots of the buildings and countryside."

"We already have something in common," Kenzie declared. "I'm also into photography. I think it'll come in handy with my major in archaeology. Not only as a scientific tool, but also as an avenue to create some interesting art."

"Hey, not to interrupt," Charlie said, breaking in, "but is there another exit from the tower?"

"Not to my knowledge. Why do you ask?" Grant inquired.

"Well, when we first got here, I glanced up at the tower and I could have sworn that I saw—"

"A woman in white standing in the window?" Grant said, finishing Charlie's sentence.

"Yeah. How did you know?" Charlie asked with a confused look.

"As I understand it, the tower's wall was a sealed crypt containing several well-preserved mummified bodies. One of the discovered bodies was a perfect match for the woman in white. The remains were that of a small, thin woman. It's believed that she died of a broken heart and that she roams the passageways of the tower," Grant concluded.

"And by the way, you didn't happen to pass a monk on your way back down the stairs, did you?" Kenzie asked with raised eyebrows.

"No. Why? Did you see a monk coming out of the building before we exited the tower?" Riley asked, confused by the question. The smiles the twins exchanged was answer enough.

"So, am I to assume that the monk is also a ghost?" Riley inquired, already knowing their response.

"Bingo! Long story short, Robert de Montrose was a prior at St. Andrews Cathedral. He was known to be a good guy, always protecting his fellow man. He was also a strict disciplinarian. One of the misbehaved monks didn't like being punished, so he murdered Robert and threw his body off the tower. So, now Robert's ghost can be found lurking in the stairway leading up to the tower. He's said to help guide people so they don't end up going over the edge like he did," Kenzie ended, waiting for a reaction from their friends.

"Oh, great! More ghosts!" Charlie uttered under his breath. At that moment, Grant and Kenzie were distracted by some friends across the yard and walked over to say hi.

"You know, Riley, most guys like to claim that they're chick magnets. But me, oh no, my claim to fame is being a ghost magnet," Charlie complained to his cousin with a disgruntled frown that distorted his handsome face.

"I don't think that ghosts are all that you attract," Riley said with an impish grin. She glanced over at Kenzie. Before Charlie had a chance to respond, the twins were back.

"Now, where were we? Oh yeah, well, enough talk about ghosts," Grant declared. "Where to next?"

"We'd love to see more of St. Andrews, but first, how do the two of you feel about solving a mystery?" Riley asked, unable to hide the excitement in her voice. Riley and Charlie recounted the theft of the amulet, and when they had finished, both Grant and Kenzie were enthusiastically on board.

"If anybody would know about the theft, it would be our archaeology professor, Kendrick Abernathy. He's been a professor at the university for decades, and he is an expert in antiquities," Kenzie suggested. The rest of the group agreed to the idea and set off toward the university in search of the professor. As they turned to leave, Charlie caught a glimpse of a woman in white coming out from behind the tower.

So, I guess there was another exit, Charlie thought, relieved that ghosts weren't going to be joining him on this trip.

Chapter Four

An Unusual Meeting with Professor Abernathy

The foursome found Professor Abernathy in the research lab. His head was bent over a microscope as he was totally engrossed in the object that he was scrutinizing under the lens.

"Excuse me, Professor Abernathy, would it be possible for us to have a word with you?" Grant asked. The professor turned to greet his visitors. The man standing before them appeared to be in his early seventies. He had a slender, muscular build. His tanned, weathered skin was in sharp contrast to his snow-white hair, which had been captured in a ponytail at the nape of his neck. He welcomed his unexpected guests with a smile and a warm handshake as Grant introduced him to Riley and Charlie.

The cousins were in awe of the many artifacts that surrounded them. The walls were lined with cupboards and cabinets. Glass cases in the center of the room displayed pieces of broken pottery, rocks, flint tools, and bones from various living creatures. Several worktables housed microscopes and computers. Petri dishes containing seashells, rocks, and other small, dated artifacts were scattered on tables throughout the room. Pictures of dig sites hung on the walls opposite the cupboards.

"Well then. What can I do for you?" the professor asked, sitting down on one of the stools. Riley relayed the story told to them by Ms. Macpherson.

"So, we were wondering if you have any other information about the amulet?" Riley asked. Professor Abernathy ran his hand across the top of his head. A perplexed expression deepened the creases in his face.

"This is a bit curious," he answered, getting up from the stool and walking over to one of the computers. "Just this morning I was checking the history on my computer, and I saw that someone had searched for that exact same artifact. The only one who was in my office prior to my search was Kalen, the foreman who's working on the renovation. He had been waiting to speak to me about a request I made regarding extra storage space. I can't imagine that he would have any interest in the amulet. What are the chances that after nearly a century there'd be this sudden interest? Although, come to think of it, we did have a thistle festival a few weeks ago."

The professor paused. "Now that you mention it, I remember seeing a headline regarding the theft as I scanned the local paper. I don't recall any of the particulars. I haven't much time for slogging through the news. An article like that could create a buzz and get people itching to find a lost treasure," he remarked. "Anyway. I'm sorry. I can't add any more details to what you already know."

"Are there any cliffs around here?" asked Charlie. "Ms. Macpherson suggested that maybe Lars chose to climb up the rocks, lost his footing, slipped, and fell into the sea. And if that's the case, then the amulet could be buried under sand, rocks, and debris near or around the cliffs."

"The closest cliffs are the sandstone cliffs located at Kinkell Braes, about a mile and a half from here," offered the professor. At that moment a student came through the door.

"Pardon me, Professor Abernathy. I don't mean to interrupt, but we have an appointment to review the next phase of my project," the young man remarked.

"Of course. Come in. Let me introduce you to these folks. Kinsey and Grant are students enrolled in my advanced summer archaeology program. And these are their friends Riley and Charlie. This is Barclay Adair. He has an internship at the university in archaeology. He's quite the talented young man. It was our good fortune to have been able to entice him away from the archaeology department at the Museum of

Edinburgh," the professor said, giving Barclay a smile and a nod.

"Nice to meet you," Barclay replied. "But I'm really the fortunate one. Professor Abernathy is an incredible mentor."

"We'd better get going," Grant suggested. "We don't want to stand in the way of the next major discovery. Thank you for your input, Professor. We appreciate you taking the time to see us."

Once the four detectives were out of the building, they reflected on the meeting with Barclay and the professor.

"OK. Don't you think it quite a coincidence that someone was researching the amulet that went missing from, ah, where? … Oh, yeah, the museum in Edinburgh. And that Barclay Adair just happened to have worked at that same museum?" Riley asked, her analytical mind already creating pieces of a puzzle that would hopefully lead to the bigger picture. "And did you notice Barclay's accent?" She looked for feedback from the others.

"It sounded Norwegian to me," Kenzie responded. "He might be an exchange student. Why is that important?"

"It might not be. But sometimes it's the little things we miss that turn out to be the most important," Riley hypothesized.

"So, what's next?" Grant asked, eager to proceed with their investigation. "Kinsey and I are in class for the better part of the day tomorrow. Professor Abernathy's teaching assistant, Colin Balfour, will be demonstrating the fine art of excavation. Who knows, this hands-on demonstration just might come in handy in our probe for clues."

"While you and Kenzie are in class, Charlie and I will hit the library and try to dig up any information that has been reported surrounding the discovery of Lars's body. The local account of the story might include details that Ms. Macpherson either didn't know or neglected to share," Riley proposed.

"Let's plan to meet after your class. We can share any information that we have unearthed. Unearthed. Get it? A little archaeological pun there, guys," Charlie joked. A collective groan was the response to his weak attempt at humor. *I guess that didn't score any points with Kenzie,* he thought. *I should probably do away with the corny jokes.*

Now that a plan of action had been determined, Grant and Kenzie suggested that they take their friends on a brief tour of St. Andrews to show them the location of the library. On their way, they passed the St. Andrews Museum.

Hmm, there's another possible source for our research, Riley thought.

The cousins arrived home in time to help Mom get dinner on the table.

"So, how did everyone's first day go?" Dad asked, looking around the table.

"The botanic gardens were spectacular!" Mom raved. "I spent several hours walking around the grounds until I found the perfect subject for my next masterpiece." She laughed. "What about you two? How did sightseeing go with Kenzie and Grant?" The teens exchanged a covert glance.

"Ah, great! We climbed Rule's Tower, saw a ghost, then went on to the university, where we were introduced to Professor Abernathy, the twins' archaeology instructor," Riley answered.

"Grant pointed out the location of the library. So, Riley and I thought we'd check out the internet," Charlie added. "Oh, and let's please nix the ghost part of the story! Although, from what we've heard, St. Andrews is a haven for apparitions."

"What about you, Dad? How was your first day on the job?" Riley inquired.

"It went well. Although it's going to be a tricky process because of the old stone that must be removed before they can begin. Luckily, the renovation crew has an excellent reputation and is open to suggestions. Oh! And speaking of old stone, you'll never guess what I came across during my inspection. Several of the stones had a picture of a thistle etched into them. The stones must have been removed, etched, then recemented. You can tell because the mortar is a different color. I noticed that one stone had cracks in the mortar all the way around it, almost as if it had been removed and then put back in place. I didn't have an opportunity to examine it closer because I was interrupted by Professor Abernathy and one of the interns working in the science building. Apparently, they were curious about the renovations," Dad concluded.

"Did you catch the intern's name?" Charlie asked, looking over at Riley.

"Let's see. Yes. I think that he said his name was Barclay," Dad answered, nodding his head. "Any reason you asked?"

"No. I was just wondering," Charlie replied.

Chapter Five

Secrets

Right after breakfast, the family went their separate ways. Riley and Charlie made a beeline for the library on North Haugh. When they entered the building, they were surprised by the atmosphere. Students were socializing, eating, and drinking, as well as studying. They walked up to the main desk and asked where they might go to research information housed in the archives. They were directed to the third floor. When they reached the third floor, they were met with silence.

"This is more like it," Riley whispered, walking over to the librarian who was sitting at the desk. "Excuse me. Where would we find St. Andrews newspapers from 1932?"

The librarian escorted them to a separate room. Once inside, she explained the filing system, then left.

"Well, let's have at it," Charlie said, pulling out a stack of newspapers preserved in plastic sleeves.

Meanwhile, Kenzie and Grant were meeting with Colin Balfour, Professor Abernathy's teaching assistant, for their first hands-on lesson in the field.

"Kinsey and I are eager to try out our excavation techniques," Grant announced, rubbing his hands together. "Where's our first dig?"

"We're going to start out at a previous excavation site, a place called Kinkell Braes. The location lies at the foot of some sandstone cliffs. No one has worked the grounds for over a hundred years. It's the perfect area to hone your skills without disturbing potential artifacts," Colin answered. Then he began gathering tools necessary for the lesson.

"We were just discussing the cliffs with our friends. Did you ever hear anything about a man by the name of Lars Eriksson? We heard that he was the prime suspect for the theft of the thistle amulet stolen from the museum in Edinburgh in 1932," Kenzie probed.

"Now that you mention it, the story does sound familiar. Wasn't his body found washed ashore several miles away from the cliffs? I can't remember the exact details. Didn't they think he was trying to escape by boat, and it capsized? I don't believe the amulet was ever found. Why are you so interested in an event that happened almost a century ago? Are you hoping to unearth the exquisite amethyst- and emerald-bejeweled treasure during your time here at the university?" Colin laughed.

"Fat chance of that ever happening." Grant laughed. "We'll be happy just to find a cracked piece of pottery or some old rusty tool."

As the twins followed Colin out to the truck, something about the way Colin described the amulet struck Grant as odd. *It seems a bit strange for someone who claims to know so little about the theft to give such a vivid description of the amulet. This would be the perfect position for someone to search for the artifact under the guise of being a teacher's assistant,* Grant theorized. *Any future information we find will be kept between Riley, Charlie, Kenzie, and me.*

After several hours of scanning newspaper articles back at the library with no luck, Riley and Charlie were ready to call it quits.

"I've had it. My eyes are going crossed," Charlie complained, rubbing his sockets. Riley agreed. She began gathering the remaining papers when an article at the bottom of the page caught her eye.

"Look!" she cried, pointing to the words in dark print: "Body Found Washed Ashore." The article contained all the information Ms. Macpherson had shared, except for two new facts: an abandoned car belonging to Lars had been found parked near the foot of Kinkell Braes sandstone cliffs that overlook the North Sea, and there was an autopsy report. The coroner had found multiple contusions and fractures to the skull, which might have resulted from a serious fall from a considerable height.

"So, if that car belonged to Lars, it must mean that he had been somewhere around the cliffs," Riley surmised. She handed Charlie the newspapers to be placed back in the file cabinet. Charlie checked his watch.

"Grant and Kenzie should be out of class by now. Let's catch up with them and update them on what we uncovered," Charlie suggested. As Riley and Charlie turned to leave, they saw Barclay staring at them through the glass door.

"Hello there. Now what are the chances that we'd run into each other again so soon?" Charlie remarked.

"I was dropping off some documents for Professor Abernathy when I saw you through the window. Thought I'd hang around and say hi. What are you two researching?" Barclay asked.

"We're delving into St. Andrews history. Charlie and I thought it would be interesting to see what made news decades ago," Riley said, hoping that her explanation sounded genuine.

"Any luck uncovering anything shocking?" Barclay inquired.

"Not really. Look at the time!" Charlie said, glancing down at his watch. "We'd better get moving. We're meeting friends in a few minutes. It was nice seeing you again, Barclay." After a quick goodbye, the cousins were out the door.

They were acting a bit strange, Barclay thought. *I wonder what they were really researching?*

Riley and Charlie arrived just in time to meet the twins as they were unloading their excavation gear from Colin's truck. Grant introduced the cousins to the professor's teaching assistant. After the equipment was stored, the foursome bid Colin farewell and headed toward St. Salvator's Quad, eager to share what they had discovered. As they approached the quad, Riley and Charlie noticed that several students were purposely avoiding stepping on some stones that formed the letters *PH.*

"So, what's their issue with the stones?" Charlie asked.

"So, what's their issue with the stones?" Charlie asked, watching students cautioning others to walk around the bricks.

"OK, here's the story. In the year 1528, Patrick Hamilton, a young man twenty-four years of age, was burned alive. He was charged as a heretic because he followed the teachings of Martin Luther. The doctrine preached by Hamilton threatened the archbishop. Hamilton was tried and executed on the same day as the trial. Due to damp wood, several attempts to ignite the fire failed. Gunpowder was placed under his arms, which resulted in severe injuries. Hamilton's torment lasted for six hours before he finally succumbed to the flames. Before he died, he condemned Alexander Campbell, the Black Friar, for betraying him. Campbell died from a mysterious illness a few days later. If you look upward at St. Salvator's church tower, you'll see what appears to be Hamilton's face burned into the brick. So, this area is cursed.

"If you look upward, you'll see what appears to be Hamilton's face burned into the brick."

If a student steps on the stones forming the letters *PH*, then that student will fail his or her finals. Whether one believes in the curse or not, no one is willing to take the risk," Grant concluded.

"Don't tell me: Hamilton's ghost is lurking around every corner, right?" Charlie queried, looking up at the tower.

"Nope. No roaming ghosts to worry about," Kenzie reassured him. "At least not here."

"Wait until you hear what we learned about Lars from the newspaper," Riley interjected. "Not much of a segue, I guess." She laughed. Riley shared what they had uncovered about the car and the possible cause of Lars's death.

"Our turn," Kinsey chimed in. "You'll never believe the location of our first dig site! We're excavating an old archaeological plot at the foot of the Kinkell Braes cliffs. Given the information you and Charlie found and the area Grant and I are examining, well, the overlap can't be just a coincidence. It appears to me that unforeseen forces are all pointing to the same direction."

"The cliffs!" the three newly self-appointed detectives replied in unison. They all agreed that Kinkell Braes was ground zero for the investigation. Because of the time, the four teens decided to meet at the cliffs the following afternoon.

"By the way, how are the excavation lessons coming along? Find anything interesting?" Charlie asked.

"It's tedious work. First, we had to make a grid. Then we painstakingly began to loosen the soil with a variety of small picks. When we came across something solid, we used brushes to carefully sweep away the earth into the dustpan. It's an extremely slow process. It's certainly not a career for someone lacking patience." Grant sighed, shaking his head.

"Fingers crossed that tomorrow's excursion will be a bit more exciting. Hopefully we'll find a clue that will give us some insight into what might have happened to Lars the day he died," Riley suggested, smiling at Grant and giving him a pat on his shoulder.

Later that evening, over dinner, the family shared their day's activities. When it was their turn, the cousins briefed Riley's parents about the trip to the library, purposely omitting the investigation in the archives. They assured the adults that the excursions were uneventful, harmless—nothing to worry about.

"Happy to hear that the two of you are sticking to sightseeing instead of sleuthing." Dad laughed, shaking his head, as he glanced over at his wife with a skeptical expression. Both Riley and Charlie were extremely eager to hear about Dad's project.

"Quick! Dad, please tell us about what you found behind the stone marked with a thistle," Riley begged. "Was there some kind of treasure or ancient artifact?"

"There seems to be an abundance of interest in what might have been concealed in the gap behind the rock. After I had shared the mystery of the missing amulet, Kalen, our foreman, was champing at the bit to extract the stone and get a sneak peek inside. I'm sorry to report that after all the anticipation, the cupboard was bare. Although it would have been the perfect place to stow away something of value until the owner returned to retrieve it in the future," Dad concluded apologetically. It was obvious by the disappointed expressions on the teens' faces that they had been hoping for something a bit more exciting.

"So, maybe Lars hid the amulet in the wall in case the authorities suspected him. That way he wouldn't have it in his possession until he was ready to flee the country," Riley surmised.

"It's a great theory, Detective Boyle," Dad said. "I guess we'll never know exactly what transpired."

After dinner, Riley and Charlie helped with the cleanup, then headed outside with Riley's parents for a few games of croquet.

Chapter Six

Coincidence or Mystic Intervention?

The following morning, Grant and Kenzie stopped by the house to pick up Riley and Charlie on their way to the Kinkell Braes sandstone cliffs. Hoping to get some unique shots of the sandstone formations, both girls brought cameras. The foursome headed down the street on their way to the cliffs, hoping that they might uncover a clue or at least some sign indicating that Lars had visited the cliffs. Grant and Riley led the way while deep in conversation. It appeared from their demeanor that they were enjoying each other's company. Evidently, Kenzie had overlooked Charlie's lame jokes and was getting a kick out of his witty repartee. When they arrived at their destination, the twins guided Riley and Charlie over to their archaeological dig and gave them a quick demonstration of a few methods used to uncover buried artifacts. Riley snapped a picture of the site for posterity.

"OK. Who's ready to tackle this puppy?" Charlie challenged. He found a foothold and started his ascent. The others followed, making sure to carefully secure each foot before stepping up to the next crevice.

"Keep an eye out for any sign that Lars was once on this cliff," Charlie ordered. "Like it was only about ninety-eight years ago. Should be a no-brainer." He laughed.

When the group finally reached the summit, they were winded, but it was worth it. The view of the North Sea was breathtaking.

"Time to take some photos," Riley suggested, pulling her camera from its case, removing the lens cap, then carefully slipping the camera strap over her shoulder. After taking several pictures of the water, she turned to capture the shoreline with its tall native grasses and beautiful pink wildflowers, all set against a backdrop of jagged stone. Riley's next step proved to be a disaster.

As she was snapping pictures of the rugged terrain, she slipped on a loose stone, causing her to lose her balance. Her camera flew up in the air and careened down the side of the cliff. Grant was able to grab Riley's wrist just as she was going over the side. Riley was able to grasp onto a limb protruding from a fissure in the stone. Luckily, there was a ledge below her feet, which helped her secure her position.

Riley's next step proved to be a disaster.

"Are you all right?" Charlie yelled, gazing down at his cousin.

"I'm OK," Riley answered in a shaky voice. "Meet me at the bottom. I can ease my way down from here." As she began her slow descent down the cliff, something shiny wedged into a crevice in the rock caught her attention. She shifted her body to get a closer look. She reached into the opening and began to slowly pull on the object until her fingers had a good grip. When she finally extracted the item, she noticed that it was a chain and pendant.

Riley clutched the necklace tight in her hand until she reached the bottom of the cliff.

That was a close call! A fall from that height could have been fatal, thought the concealed observer who was witnessing the accident from a distance.

"Let me check you out," Kenzie insisted, already giving Riley the once-over. "Does anything hurt? It doesn't look like anything's broken. You do have some scrapes that will need tending to."

"I'm fine thanks to your brother. The outcome could have been entirely different if Grant hadn't caught me and broken the fall," Riley replied, giving Grant an affectionate smile. Seeing that his cousin was not seriously injured, Charlie went over to the base of the cliffs and retrieved Riley's camera. It was amazing that the camera had sustained very little damage.

"Oh my! Oh my! Is she OK?" Professor Abernathy cried as he hurried onto the scene. "I was checking on the dig Colin was conducting with Grant and Kenzie when I saw the fall."

"I'm in one piece—just a few scrapes," Riley answered. *Boy, the professor is sure spry for his age. He made it over here in record time,* Riley thought, discreetly tucking the necklace in her jeans pocket. *Best to keep this between the four of us for the time being until we learn its significance.*

After the professor left, Riley removed the chain from her pocket and showed it to the others. The silver chain and pendant were tarnished. Upon closer examination, the teens could make out a symbol on the lavaliere. It appeared to be an ornate decorative hammer.

"So, I guess our next step is to research the meaning of the fancy hammer," Charlie suggested. "Quite sure that it has nothing to do with pounding in nails. Let's get you home, Riley, and cleaned up. We'll save the investigating for tomorrow."

"You can hold on to me." Grant offered his arm to Riley to steady her.

Their curiosity regarding the amulet may have turned up something. My gut instinct told me to keep an eye on them. I'm sure glad I did, he thought, already plotting his next move.

Once the cousins were home, the twins said their goodbyes.

"Kenzie and I will catch up with you tomorrow," Grant called back over his shoulder. "Hopefully this discovery will lead to something. If not, you have a new piece of used Scottish jewelry." He laughed.

* * *

"Goodness gracious! What on earth happened to you, sweetheart?" Mom cried when Riley limped into the room. Riley explained the events that led up to the accident, omitting one crucial fact, namely, why they were there in the first place. She did show her parents what she had found deep in the crevice of the cliff.

"From now on, maybe you should keep both feet planted firmly on the ground," Dad suggested. "Remember the trouble the two of you ran into climbing cliffs in Maine? At least this time you weren't involved in any mysterious conspiracy theory." Dad sighed in relief. The teens avoided exchanging glances for fear it would give away their secret. After all, this could all lead to nowhere.

Meanwhile, on the way back to the dorm, Kenzie and her brother were in conversation.

"My hero! You're so brave and strong," Kenzie teased as she gazed up into her brother's eyes, batting her eyelashes, pretending to be Riley.

"Knock it off, Kenzie!" Grant barked, giving his sister a gentle punch on the arm. "I just reacted. Thank goodness Riley wasn't seriously injured."

"You're right, Brother. But I really do believe that you have won her heart in some sort of heroic way. Just sayin'," Kenzie, stated, returning a loving punch.

"Oh yeah, and what about you and Charlie? It's obvious that you enjoy his company. You even laugh at his cheesy jokes. And he appears to be extremely interested in everything that you have to say," Grant quipped.

"No comment!" was Kenzie's curt reply. The two continued in silence, each reflecting on their conversation.

Chapter Seven

Prying Eyes

The following morning, the four friends were en route to the library to uncover the origin of the ornate hammer. Kenzie suggested that they take a walk down Market Street and check out the many cafes and shops.

"Sounds like a plan. I could go for some hot chocolate and a scone," Charlie answered, demonstrating what little knowledge he had of Scottish cuisine.

After treating themselves to a delicious snack, they were ready to hit the library. The foursome was unaware of the individual watching them from the cafe across the street.

OK. Where are they headed next? the onlooker wondered. *I saw the girl put something in her pocket after she climbed down from the cliff yesterday. What are the chances that it could have something to do with a heist committed years ago? But from what I've heard, that seems to be the driving force behind their excursions. Keeping a close eye on them may prove to be profitable.* The nefarious individual snickered diabolically.

The four teens made their way up to the third floor of the library. Here it was quiet, and no one would overhear what they were discussing. It didn't take long to find the unique hammer.

It appeared to be an ornate decorative hammer.

"I think we're on to something!" Riley whispered, unable to contain her excitement. "It all fits! Lars was from Norway.

In Norse mythology, Thor was a god representing strength, along with having many other attributes. Thor's hammer is depicted on a variety of items, especially jewelry."

"So," Grant said, interrupting, "it makes sense that if Lars climbed to the top of the cliffs for whatever reason, he could have slipped, kind of like you did, Riley, and somehow lost his necklace."

"And from that point it was all down-cliff for poor old Lars." Charlie laughed. A collective muted groan was shared by the other members of the party.

"Hey! What can I say? When you got it, you got it!" Charlie added with a shrug.

"What's our next step?" Kenzie asked. "You two are the expert detectives, and you have a limited amount of time here. I think we need a cohesive plan of action so that we're not spinning our wheels."

"Charlie and I will put our heads together this afternoon while you're at class. Why don't you stop by after dinner? Hopefully we'll have something to share. Oh, and Kenzie, how about bringing your camera? We can check out the pictures we took yesterday before I decided to go cliff diving," Riley suggested.

Earlier that morning while the teens were on their secret mission, Dad was at work supervising the rough carpentry work for the new addition. He was in the middle of discussing a major change with the carpenter when Kalen came rushing over.

"Morning, Donald. How's your daughter doing?" Kalen asked with a look of concern.

"She's fine. Just a few scrapes on her arms and legs," Dad replied. "Why do you ask?" Dad was somewhat confused by Kalen's knowledge of the accident. "And how did you know that she was my daughter?"

"I had a couple of hours to spare, so I took a walk up to Kinkell Braes to take in the scenery. I love sitting by the water. Helps a guy to clear his head. Anyway, as I was enjoying the view, I heard someone cry out. I looked over in the direction of the cry, and that's when I noticed a young woman climbing down the side of the cliff. When she got to the bottom, Professor Abernathy rushed over, and it appeared to me that the professor and the girl's friends were checking her over for possible injuries," Kalen explained. "I caught up with the professor to ask how the young lady was doing. After he reassured me that her injuries weren't serious, he explained that she was your daughter. So then, how's your young mountain goat doing today?"

"Well, she's none the worse for wear." Dad laughed. "Although she did find something interesting on her rock-climbing adventure. Seems that someone lost a necklace. Riley found the weathered piece of jewelry wedged in a crack. So, I guess the scrapes were worth it. Now she has a souvenir from

Scotland. She certainly seemed thrilled about finding that old dirt-encrusted necklace. Kids! There's no telling what's going to excite them." Dad turned to continue his conversation with the carpenter. Kalen headed over to the bench to grab some tools.

"By the way, Kalen, thanks for asking." Kalen turned and gave Dad a thumbs-up.

Later that evening, Grant and Kenzie joined the cousins for a quick game of croquet. The four sleuths didn't want to raise any suspicion about their agenda.

"My dear Sherlock, do we have a master plan yet?" Grant whispered to Riley.

"Still working on possibilities," Riley answered in hushed tones. "Why don't we go in and pull up the photos from yesterday? I'm anxious to see how they turned out."

The four teens gathered in the living room as Riley started scrolling through her photos on the small screen. There were just a few from yesterday. Everyone agreed that the shots of the North Sea were spectacular.

The next picture gave the four viewers quite a jolt! In the distance, not too far away from the cliffs, there appeared to be someone hiding among the tall grasses. Given that little could be seen of the individual, it was difficult to tell whether it was a man or a woman. Either way, it meant trouble. The next photo must have been snapped as the camera tumbled down the cliffs. It was a partial image of someone leaning against a tree. Again, as in the previous picture, it was impossible to distinguish the gender.

"Guys, I think that we might have made two new friends," Charlie remarked tongue-in-cheek. "Someone knows, or thinks they know, something about what we're up to. After Riley's and my last encounter with shady characters, we found that it can get dicey. Keep your eyes open, and be careful. Let's put this probe on the back burner for a couple of days. Hopefully, that will throw whoever is watching us off the track." Everyone thought it was a good idea to table their investigation for the time being.

Chapter Eight

More Pieces to the Puzzle

The next morning at breakfast, the family decided to do some sightseeing. Dad had the day off, and he said it would be nice to do something together. After considering several options, they decided to take a walk down Market Street and explore some of the shops to take in the local flavor. Riley pointed out the charming little cafe where she, Charlie, and the twins had eaten the other day. It was agreed the group would stop back for a taste of Scotland on the way home.

A visit to two of the local museums was on their itinerary. St. Andrews Heritage was a small museum situated in a seventeenth-century house with reconstructed Victorian shops and Great-Granny's Washhouse. In the rear of the museum was a lovely hidden garden with an array of gorgeous plants and exhibits.

St. Andrews Museum located in Kinburn Park was their next attraction. Upon their arrival, the foursome headed in different directions. It was no surprise that Mom gravitated toward the art gallery exhibition. Dad was drawn to the architectural displays. Riley and Charlie wanted to learn more about the subject matter that their new friends were studying, so they headed off to the archaeological arm of the museum.

As they were passing by an open door marked Receiving, Authorized Personnel Only, the sound of hushed, angry voices caused Riley to pause. She put her finger to her lips, signaling for her cousin to keep still.

"I can't go along with this! You don't realize what you're asking me to do. You're putting me in an impossible position," a woman whispered, barely able to maintain her composure.

"It's not forever," a man's voice countered. "You're here for, what, three months? That should be plenty of time to accomplish our goal."

"Let's get it straight! It's your goal, not mine!" she snapped. She stormed out of the room, nearly running into Riley. "Oh, I'm so sorry." Just then things registered for Ms. Macpherson. "Oh my! You're the cousins from the United States. We met in at the museum in Edinburgh. What a coincidence! So, how are you enjoying your stay in St. Andrews?" She tried to appear calm.

"It's amazing! It's like walking into a *Harry Potter* movie. We've made some friends, and they've been showing us around the campus. We've also been alerted to beware of some of the ghosts that reside in the area," Riley offered.

"That sounds a bit unnerving," Ms. Macpherson replied with a grimace. "The Scottish do have their fair share of spirits, so I'd heed the warning." She tried to keep from smiling. "So, can I help you find something?"

"We're on our way to the archaeological exhibit," Charlie answered.

"Well, you're headed in the right direction. Just continue down this hallway and turn right. You can't miss it," she replied, then hurried away down the corridor.

"I wonder what that was all about?" Charlie asked.

"Yeah. It sounded intense. I'd like to know who Ms. Macpherson was talking to," Riley added. "Anyway, we'd better get going before Mom and Dad come looking for us." She moved away from the door.

As Riley rounded the corner, she happened to glance back over her shoulder just in time to see Barclay emerge from the Authorized Personnel room. "Hey, Charlie, you'll never guess who Ms. Macpherson was arguing with," Riley challenged.

"So, spill. Who was it?" Charlie urged.

"Barclay," she whispered. "I wonder what he wants Ms. Macpherson to do that has her so upset? So many questions, yet so few answers. It'll be interesting to hear what Grant and Kenzie think."

While Riley's family was taking in the sights, Grant and Kenzie were preparing for their next dig. Grant had loaded most of the gear in the truck. He was going back for the last few items when Colin called him over.

"Hey, Grant, when you go back into the lab, could you please bring me the plans for today's excavation? I think I left them folded on the bookshelf marked 'Archaeology 101.' If you do that, then I can finish securing the equipment and we can get going," urged Colin.

"No problem. I'll get right on it, Mr. Balfour," Grant answered as he headed back to the building. Grant gathered the rest of the implements he needed then went in search of the prints. He walked over to the shelf labeled "Archaeology 101," but there were no papers in sight. *OK, I know this is where he said I should find the plans, but unless they're invisible, they're not here. So then, where else can they be?* Grant wondered. He began looking through the overhead cupboards that housed books once used for research. He was about to give up when he spotted some folded sheets of paper sticking out of one of the books. *Finally! Mr. Balfour will think that I got lost.* He felt somewhat exasperated. Grant opened the paperwork to make sure that this was what his instructor wanted.

Well, this certainly doesn't look like an excavation site plan. These are recent invoices for antiquities delivered to the St. Andrews Museum. Why would someone stick these statements in an old book? Grant pondered. Then he replaced the paperwork back where he had found it. At that moment, Colin came bustling into the room.

"Caught you in the nick of time, before you had searched the entire room. Sorry to have sent you on a wild-goose chase," he said. "I found the site work in the back seat of the truck. I must have put it in there the other day so that I wouldn't forget it. So much for having a mind like a steel trap." He laughed as he headed toward the door. Grant picked up the remaining tools and followed the instructor out to the truck.

I'm anxious to share this latest bit of info with the rest of the group, Grant thought, wondering how they'd react.

When Colin, Kenzie, and Grant arrived at the site, they were shocked to find the entire roped-off area in disarray. The ropes were haphazardly cast aside and lay in a tangled pile. The once level earth was disheveled, creating a moonscape appearance with its pockmarked holes and mountains of dirt. The three looked at one another in disbelief.

"Who could have done this, and why?" Kenzie asked, turning to Colin, hoping for a reasonable answer.

"I have no idea. Maybe this was some sort of an initiation prank. Whatever it was, it's totally unacceptable!" Colin snapped. "People in the area know that excavation digs are off-limits to the public. It's not a law, but the community has always shown respect for the work being done here. This is a first!" He snarled angrily.

"I have an idea," Kenzie offered. "It's just a theory. When we met Professor Abernathy, he thought that the sudden interest in the amulet might be the result of the Thistle Festival and an article resurrecting the details of the robbery. So now someone in the town is in search of the beloved treasure."

"I guess anything's possible." Colin shrugged. "It seems to me that it would be like looking for a needle in a haystack. For all I know, the amulet could be at the bottom of the sea. Now, let's get back to the task at hand."

"What do you want us to do?" Grant asked. He began gathering and organizing the assemblage of ropes.

"We'll set up another site just beyond the curve in the cliff. It's a bit more secluded with less foot traffic," Colin suggested. "It's going to set us back time-wise. Do you mind helping me set up the grid? That way we can start first thing in the morning."

The twins agreed to lend a hand. As Grant was kneeling, staking out the far end of the grid, he noticed a chisel partially hidden in the grass. He held up the item for Colin to see.

"Is this a tool we'll be using later on?" Grant asked. "I found it here in the grass. Maybe it belongs to the excavation raider or raiders from last night." Colin looked over and laughed.

"Not unless you're planning on carving a likeness of your face into the sandstone cliff, you know, like the one in the United States with the presidents."

"You mean Mount Rushmore. Don't hold your breath." Grant chuckled.

Meanwhile, after an informative visit to the museum, Riley's family had worked up an appetite. It was time for some nourishment. As they left the museum, heading to the cafe, they got turned around and found themselves on North Street. They proceeded down the street and eventually stumbled upon Bibis Café, a delightful eatery set in a rustic stone building with an eye-catching turquoise-blue sign.

"This looks interesting," exclaimed Mom. "Want to give it a try?" She began looking for the group's approval.

"I'm starving!" Charlie announced. "This place looks great!" As the family entered the cafe, they were greeted with a warm hello by a lovely hostess who escorted them to a table. The cafe was bright and cheerful with old-world decor. After perusing the menu, Mom and Dad ordered the smoked salmon. Riley and Charlie had decided on what the menu described as tasty chicken soup. Dessert consisted of scones and hot chocolate.

As they ate, the family shared what they had found most interesting during their visit to the museum. Charlie and Riley had already decided not to mention the conversation they had overheard between Barclay and Macpherson. Best not to upset the applecart.

When their hot chocolate arrived, the foursome couldn't believe their eyes as the server placed the steaming mugs in front of them.

"Now this is how hot chocolate should be served!" Riley exclaimed. The drink was topped with whipped cream, marshmallows, and solid chocolate cubes, and for the pièce de résistance, there was an Oreo cookie stuck into the whipped cream—a chocolate masterpiece. After consuming the deliciously rich concoction, Dad signaled for the server to bring the check. As the family was about to leave, the waitress suggested that they visit the St. Andrews Aquarium, a local attraction located right next door to the cafe. All agreed that a tour of the aquarium would be just the thing as they could walk off the rich dessert.

They found the aquarium to be a magical underwater kingdom set in the cliffs overlooking St. Andrews Bay, with more than one hundred twenty species on show. The foursome got up close and personal with sharks, octopi, crocodiles, and the ever-popular Humboldt penguins.

"This aquarium was amazing!" Riley raved as they exited the building. "I loved those feisty marmosets. They were adorable!"

"Oh yes. So adorable," Charlie mimicked, teasing his cousin.

"I'm glad our waitress recommended the tour. It was worth seeing," Mom replied. "Is everyone ready to head back to the cottage? I'm looking forward to putting my feet up and relaxing."

While the family was touring St. Andrews, an unwelcomed guest had paid them a visit. The unsavory individual had been scoping out the house on and off for a few days. The yard was secluded, which made it easy to access without being seen. He had waited for the family to leave, then he went to work.

There! The listening device is all set, the intruder thought, stepping back for a moment to admire his handiwork. The miniature gadget was hidden outside, beneath the patio table. *I've seen the four of them with their heads together when the parents weren't around, as if they've got some big secret. It's imperative that I glean some insight into what they might have discovered. I don't need them throwing a monkey wrench into what I've accomplished so far. It's bad enough that the dad is working close by. Now I have these nosy teens poking around and asking questions. Hopefully, the scene I staged will send them down a rabbit hole. For their sake, I hope it has nothing to do with my agenda.* He snarled under his breath as he hurried out of the yard.

Chapter Nine

Devising a Strategy

Grant and Kenzie caught up with the cousins after dinner. While Mom was looking through her recent sketches, deciding on which one to paint, and while Dad was reviewing a change in the project, the teens felt this was the perfect time to share what they had discovered during the day. They headed outside for a game of croquet and played for a while making small talk so they wouldn't draw undue attention. After what seemed enough time, the four gathered around the table, eager to exchange information. Riley was up first.

"OK, here goes. Charlie and I were on our way to the archaeological exhibit. As we were passing by an open door marked Receiving, we overheard a heated exchanged between Barclay and Ms. Macpherson."

"Who's Ms. Macpherson?" Grant asked.

"Oh, that's right, you don't know about Ms. Macpherson. She's the curator at the museum in Edinburgh. We met her when we visited the museum upon our arrival in Edinburgh. She's the person who told us about the theft of the amulet. Now she's acting curator at the St. Andrews Museum. And from part of the conversation that we overheard between Barclay and Ms. Macpherson, it appeared that Ms. Macpherson was under duress, as if she were being coerced into participating in something against her will. Now all we must do is figure out if that something has to do with the amulet," Riley stated.

"Did you two dig up anything interesting while you were in class?" Charlie asked the twins. Then, realizing what he said, he crossed his fingers, hoping they'd missed the pun.

"Not bad, Charlie," Kenzie said, reacting to his play on words. "Either your timing's getting better or you're starting to grow on me." She laughed.

"So, we have two unexplained incidents to report," Grant said with a perplexed expression. "As I was helping Colin load the equipment into the truck, he noticed that he'd forgotten the plans for today's excavation. He asked if I'd retrieve them when I went back into the building to collect the rest of the tools. After gathering the last of the equipment, I headed over to where Colin said I'd find the paperwork. When my search turned up nothing, I started looking in the overhead cupboards that housed out-of-date reference books. That's where I found folded sheets of paper sticking out of a book. I checked to see if these were the plans Colin requested.

"Now, here comes the good part. Instead of the site plans, I found these obscurely filed documents that turned out to be invoices for antiquities involving the St. Andrews Museum. I thought it strange at the time, but I was in a hurry to let Colin know that I couldn't find the day's blueprint. I put the invoices back in the book and returned the book to the shelf. Now that I think of it, I should have taken pictures with my phone just in case we'd need to reference them later." Grant's face showed a disgruntled expression.

"From the invoices, it looks like someone in the department is doing business with the museum," Charlie reasoned. "We could get in touch with Ms. Macpherson, explain that we have developed an interest in archaeological antiquities since we were introduced to the subject through our friends, and say that we have a few questions. Do you still have her card, Riley?" Riley gave him a thumbs-up.

"I think our next course of action is for Riley and me to speak with Ms. Macpherson and see what she has to offer. You and Kenzie can go back to the classroom and take pictures of the invoices. No one should question why you're in the lab. If they do, you can say that you thought you left something in the room. You know, I wouldn't have given this a second thought if the invoices had been filed in a legitimate location.

But who sticks important documents in a book?" Charlie questioned.

"OK, that addresses the first peculiarity," Kenzie chimed in. "Let me introduce you to part two. When we got to the excavation site, it looked like several bombs had been detonated. The grid ropes were strewn everywhere, lying in disorderly heaps. The ground was a scarred with huge holes and lumpy hills of dirt. Two thoughts came to mind: either someone was playing a prank, or someone was looking for the amulet. Speaking of the amulet, when and where are we searching next?"

"May I make a suggestion?" Riley interjected. "How about tomorrow we work on the first part of our plan and see where it leads? Regarding the amulet, I think that we go back to where I found the necklace and search the area directly below that side of the cliff. Maybe you and Grant can question Colin about the previous excavation area. See if he has any information that might give us a clue if it's feasible the jewelry could be buried somewhere around the old site. What do you think?" Riley looked around at the group for some feedback. Everyone agreed that Riley's suggestions had merit. The plan was in place for the next day.

The hidden listening device picked up every word with clarity.

This is worse than I imagined! I really need to get my hands on that antiquity before they do. However, the likelihood of them unearthing the treasure is very low. Yet, they did find the necklace, so I guess anything is in the realm of possibility. Back to reality. It's imperative that, in order to protect my lucrative investments, I devise a plan that will discourage these meddlesome amateur detectives, the villainous fraudster thought.

Chapter Ten

A Chilling Threat

"What's on your agenda today?" Mom asked as she set breakfast on the table.

"Charlie and I decided to check out St. Andrew's Cathedral, then head over to the museum. Since we've been spending time with the twins, we've become quite interested in archaeology. We have some questions we'd like to ask Ms. Macpherson. Then we're planning to catch up with Grant and Kenzie for the rest of the afternoon," Riley concluded, pleased that she didn't have to stretch the truth. "How about you, Mom? What subject will have the honor of being illuminated on your canvas?" This question elicited a smile from her mother.

"Well, you know I love painting seascapes. So, I think that I'll take a walk along the sea until I find a view that speaks to me." Mom laughed.

"What about you, Uncle? Anything exciting happening with the renovation?" Charlie inquired.

"Not much, thank goodness. I guess the only incident that popped up was the mystery of the lost chisel. It seemed to have disappeared into thin air. Ergo, if that's the only dilemma I deal with, I'll be one happy architect," Dad concluded.

After breakfast, the family gathered their essentials and were out the door. As Riley and Charlie were nearing St. Andrews Cathedral, they entered Pends Street, a lovely old street that once was a vaulted entrance into the monastery. The roof and top story were gone, but walking down there, it still felt like traveling through a doorway into the past.

"This is a bit creepy," Charlie remarked, looking at his cousin for her take on their surroundings. "I can't shake the feeling that we're being followed, like someone is watching us." He moaned.

"I'm right there with you, Coz. It's like the hairs on the back of my neck are standing on end," she replied. Both she and Charlie turned around to see if anyone was sneaking up behind them. As they turned, they caught a glimpse of a wisp of fluttering black fabric trailing out of sight behind the stone wall at the far end of the street. They couldn't make out if it was a man or a woman or if he or she had been following them. But whoever or whatever it was, it left the cousins on edge.

As they turned, they caught a glimpse of a wisp of fluttering black fabric trailing out of sight behind the stone wall.

They continued on to the cathedral. Because of unsafe conditions, they were unable to enter the church, so they spent an hour or so walking around the grounds and checking out the headstones surrounding the magnificent structure.

"Hey, Charlie, did you notice the building on the left? I wonder if that woman in white is still roaming around up there in St. Rule's Tower?" Riley laughed, trying to get a rise out of her cousin.

"Very funny! Well, if she is, she can just ghost around up there. At least in Maine we only had to contend with two ghosts. Here we have the white woman, some helpful monk ghost, and poor old Patrick Hamilton. Oh yeah, and whatever was lurking about on Pends Street," Charlie shot back. "It's no wonder we're freaking out. Oh, oh, check the time! We'd better head over to the museum before we're late for our appointment."

The cousins arrived right on time for their meeting with Ms. Macpherson. She greeted them with a pleasant smile and invited them into her office.

"So, how can I help you?" she asked with a quizzical expression creasing her forehead.

"First, Charlie and I would like to thank you for taking the time for this meeting," Riley offered. "As I mentioned on the phone, we have some friends who are enrolled in an advanced summer session in Professor Abernathy's class. They've been sharing their excavation experiences with us. Since then, both Charlie and I have taken an interest in archaeology. Anyway, we were wondering how the museum obtains the artifacts on display."

"Many of our artifacts are sold on the private market. Countless private collectors have an intermediary, making these transactions in secret," Macpherson explained.

"How can you tell if the artifact you're receiving is authentic?" Charlie asked.

"There are many factors, such as material, size, shape, form, signs of age, and condition, to determine authenticity. It may take many years for items to be efficiently analyzed," she concluded.

"Do you ever buy from universities? Let's say if someone in the archaeology department unearths a relic, would the museum buy directly from the school?" Riley probed, trying to gauge the expression on Ms. Macpherson's face. She wasn't disappointed. The easy smile the curator had just worn changed dramatically.

These questions are hitting a little too close to home. I wonder if these inquiries are innocent or if these two are on to something, Ms. Macpherson pondered. Glancing at her watch, she abruptly pushed back her chair and stood up.

"I'm sorry, I have inventory arriving that I must document. I hope I was able to answer your questions adequately. By the way, have the two of you turned up any new information regarding the missing amulet?" she asked, hoping to change the subject.

"I'm afraid not. I think that ship has sailed," Charlie replied. "Unless of course our friends find it during their excavation lesson. Wouldn't that be a find for all times?" He laughed, then he and Riley followed Ms. Macpherson out of the room.

While the cousins were sightseeing and meeting with the curator, Grant, Kenzie, and Colin had arrived at the new excavation site. While Colin was unpacking the equipment, Grant went over to inspect one of the squares in the grid that appeared to have been disturbed. He carefully brushed the loosed dirt with his hand. As he was smoothing the earth, his fingers felt something just under the surface. He dug down and pulled up a piece of paper.

This is odd. Who would bury a piece of paper in our dig? Maybe this is Colin's idea of a joke, he thought as he unfolded the paper. No! This wasn't a joke. The menacing words jumped off the paper: DROP IT IF YOU KNOW WHAT'S GOOD FOR YOU! YOU'RE IN OVER YOUR HEAD! THIS IS NOT A GAME! I'M WATCHING! Grant quickly folded the paper and put it in his pocket. He'd share the note with the others later.

After unloading the excavation tools, Colin noticed that something had caught Grant's attention. Observing the troubled expression on Grant's face, Colin walked over to where his student was standing.

"What's up? Did you find something interesting?" Colin asked, looking down at the disturbed ground.

"Ah, no. I noticed that the earth in this part of the grid had been displaced, so I smoothed it over. It was probably one of those red squirrels burying a nut," Grant hypothesized, praying that his theory sounded convincing. "Before we begin our next lesson, Kenzie and I have some questions regarding the sandstone cliffs. How much erosion would occur in a hundred years?"

"That's a tough question. My research stated about two and a half centimeters. But it depends. If the period between erosion events is longer than the length of observational record, erosion risk can be underestimated," Colin explained. "Why do you ask?"

"We were just wondering how much sediment would have settled at the bottom of these cliffs on top of the previous excavation site. Say, for example, there was a large cavity left from the dig, so with the erosion of the cliffs and with the natural force of gravity eventually causing the cavity to backfill, how far down would someone have to dig to reach the old pit?" Grant inquired.

"Again, it's difficult to predict. You're not just dealing with soil. You also must consider stones and rocks that have broken off from the cliffs and then became buried in the ground. So, you might have to dig down several feet. Why all this interest in erosion? Are you thinking of changing from a career in archaeology to a career in geology?" Colin asked, trying to ascertain the twins' motives.

"No way! Studying the material remains of past human life and activities is much more interesting than analyzing the life of a rock." Kenzie laughed. "The topic came up during a conversation with our friends. They had some questions, so we thought we'd follow up with our resident expert," Kenzie schmoozed.

"For a minute there, I thought the two of you were still on the hunt for that stolen amulet. We all know that would be a foolish endeavor and a total waste of time. Now, let's get on with today's lesson. You've noticed that our grid system is based on coordinates of a fixed point that is called the datum. Our datum is a prominent geographic figure that is that boulder over there. We are going to do a vertical dig, followed by a lesson in screening. Grab your tools, and let's begin," Colin directed.

The remainder of the afternoon flew by. Riley and Charlie arrived at the university just as the excavation team was unloading the truck. Colin had an appointment, so Riley, Charlie, and the twins offered to run the equipment back to the lab. While Kenzie was putting the paraphernalia away, Grant was on a mission to document the hidden invoices with his phone. He pulled open the cupboard doors and peered inside. As he turned to face the others with the book in his hand, his shocked expression was all the explanation they needed.

"They're not here!" exclaimed Grant. "I should have taken pictures when I first found them. Now it's too late." At that moment, the office door opened, and Barclay walked in, carrying a tray containing an assortment of partially decayed bones.

"Hi, gang. Are you looking for something? Maybe I can help you. I know every inch of this room," he offered.

"No, thanks. I was just showing our friends some of the antiquated research journals while Kenzie was storing our excavating tools. Since we've met, they've taken quite an interest in archaeology. It's interesting to see how techniques have changed over the years," Grant said, returning the book to its place on the shelf and shutting the door.

"All done," Kenzie interrupted. We're good to go." The group said their goodbyes and headed out the door.

"Well, that was close!" Grant said, looking back over his shoulder. "But that's not the only thing that's unnerving. Look at what I dug up at the site." Grant pulled the threatening note from his pocket and showed it to the group.

"What did we do to cause someone to issue such a threat? It's as if this creepy individual has eyes and ears on us. We've been careful to keep this a covert operation, so I don't get it ..." Riley trailed off with a visible look of concern on her face.

"Maybe that explains why we felt a presence following us on our way to the cathedral," Charlie added. "I swear that I could sense someone's eyes penetrating my body."

"So, you must have taken Pends Street," Kenzie interjected with raised eyebrows.

"Yes. So, is there something we should know about that street?" Charlie asked, knowing that he probably wouldn't like what he was about to hear.

"As the story goes, a local girl had her heart broken after her lover's death. She mutilated herself so no man would be attracted to her ever again. She sliced off her ears, split her nostrils, branded her cheeks, and cut off her eyelids and lips. She joined the nunnery and soon after died from her injuries. Since her death, she roams Pends Street. Sometimes people have had the feeling they're being watched. Others have claimed to have seen a dark shape moving on the opposite side of the street. It has also been reported that the woman lifts her veil to others, revealing her mutilated face," Kenzie concluded.

"Oh brother. As Riley and I turned to see if someone was following us, we caught a glimpse of black fabric flowing out from behind the wall at the far end of the street. It could have been that nun. So, how many more ghostly encounters are we to expect?" Charlie questioned, sounding a bit exasperated.

"I guess it all depends on your travels," Kenzie joked, giving Charlie a comforting pat on his shoulder.

"Since we're not sure if this note is legit, I suggest that we don't take any chances. What do you think about putting trackers on our phones just in case one of us gets in trouble?" Grant suggested. "I know I must sound paranoid, but we don't know who we're dealing with."

The group approved the suggestion. After the trackers were installed, Riley and Charlie shared what they had learned from their meeting with Ms. Macpherson. The group agreed that Macpherson's behavior was suspect, but now that the invoices were missing, there was no evidence to suggest foul play.

"I think that we should focus on finding the amulet. I have an idea for an experiment that might help us narrow down the possible locations of the medallion," Riley explained. She detailed the simple procedure to her enthusiastic fellow detectives.

"It's not brain surgery, but it sounds feasible to me," Charlie responded, giving his cousin a high five. It was agreed that the four would meet at the lab the next morning after class.

Chapter Eleven

An Experiment in Trajectory

There were no additional unwanted surprises the following day, much to the twins' relief. The morning's dig progressed without interruption. Although the lesson was interesting, the twins were eager for the class to end so they could get on with the search for the lost treasure.

Riley and Charlie were waiting for their friends outside the lab when they arrived back at the science building. Professor Abernathy greeted them as they entered the room.

"Well, as I recall, the last time we met, you were extremely interested in that stolen thistle amulet. Any luck discovering further information that may help solve the mystery?" the professor asked with raised eyebrows.

"No, sir. We've come up empty," Riley fibbed. "We are now officially tourists."

"Excuse me, Professor, where's Barclay?" Grant asked. "I haven't seen him around today."

"He's researching high-tech devices that help archaeologists discover ancient sites. There's something called a muon detector that can peer inside pyramids in Egypt and into chambers beneath volcanoes. There are also space archaeology satellites that can map hundreds, if not thousands, of sites in weeks, instead of a few dozen in one summer. Pretty impressive technology, don't you agree?"

Too bad we can't get our hands on one of those devices. I bet we'd find the amulet if it's buried somewhere around the base of the cliffs, Riley thought.

"Would the university have access to either one of those devices?" Riley asked.

"No. There are several steps the department must follow before being qualified to obtain either," Abernathy replied.

"Maybe high-tech would answer the question of how deep one would have to dig to get down to the old excavation site," Colin remarked, turning to the twins. "For a while, Professor, I thought that we were going to lose our budding archaeologist to the field of geology. They had several questions regarding weathering."

"Geoarchaeologists' work frequently involves studying soil and sediments to contribute to an archaeological study. So, your questions are relevant to the field. The context of your questions leads me to believe that you're thinking of trying to reach the previous excavation site. Am I correct in making that assumption?" he asked.

"No, Professor Abernathy, absolutely not! Grant and I spend enough time digging during class." Kenzie laughed. "And I do believe our friends would rather see the sights than to burrow through the dirt to find who knows what."

"Point taken." The professor chuckled. "Now I've got to be going. I have some artifacts that need to be registered and catalogued. Enjoy your day," he said as he turned to head to his office.

"Professor, I have just one more question," Riley pressed. "We were wondering, if someone discovered a precious antiquity during an excavation conducted by the university, could the school sell it to a museum?"

"No. You see, in Scotland, all archaeological artifacts may be claimed on behalf of the Crown under common law. This applies no matter where or on whose property the artifacts are found. So, the university can't profit off the relics they discover," the professor explained. "Now I really must run." He headed to his office then exited out the back door to receive the shipment.

"Well, that's a bummer," Charlie uttered. "All that work just to have your country reap the spoils."

After checking in their equipment, the foursome headed out for the cliffs.

"So, what do you make of that latest bit of information?" Grant asked once they were out of earshot. "If the school can't benefit from their acquisitions, then what's the explanation for the invoices documenting payments to the university from the St. Andrews Museum? From what you shared with us about Ms. Macpherson's reaction to your question and the disappearing invoices, I believe something illegal is in the offing."

"I agree," Riley responded. "First things first. Let's get on with the experiment, then we'll circle back to the invoices."

When they reached the base of the cliffs, they put Riley's plan into action. Charlie, Kenzie, and Riley each collected four rocks that had the approximate weight of the amulet. Next, they climbed up to the spot where Riley had lost her footing. Grant remained on the ground to mark the area with spray paint to indicate where the rocks had landed. Charlie was the tallest, so he was given the honor of reenacting the night Lars had slipped to his death. Charlie proved to be an accomplished actor, feigning an agonized scream after the last throw.

"That certainly was entertaining." Kenzie laughed on their way down the cliff. "Now let's see where those mock amulets landed." Grant met the others at the foot of the cliff and directed them to the twelve potential burial sites.

"So, what's next?" Kenzie asked Riley, waiting for her to reveal their next steps.

"We don't want to be conspicuous, so we need to devise a plan on *when* we're going to attempt digging in these various spots. Why don't you come over after dinner and we can put our heads together? With our four brilliant minds, I'm sure we'll come up with something. I have a good feeling about this," Riley stated.

I have a good feeling about this too, mused the person observing just out of sight a few feet away. *I'm looking forward to hearing just how they're planning to pull this off.* He snickered to himself. *Apparently, they didn't take my threat too seriously. I thought they had given up playing detective when I removed the invoices. It's crystal clear from their conversation that they're not done meddling. How can four teenagers cause so much trouble? My next move must be more than just a written threat. It's imperative that they realize that their lives are in danger. I'll wait for the right opportunity to present itself. But for now, I have a treasure to find!*

Chapter Twelve

A Devastating Discovery

Later that evening, the twins arrived after dinner as planned. Riley's dad greeted them at the door.

"How's the excavation business coming along?" He laughed as he showed them in.

"It's a dirty job, but someone has to do it," Grant countered. "All kidding aside, it's extremely interesting. We haven't unearthed anything yet that will get our names in a journal, but one can always hope. Our next experience will take place at an actual untouched excavation site. So, maybe we'll get lucky. How's it going for you, Mr. Boyle? Find any more secret stone panels? It seems like there should be some sort of mystery surrounding that ancient basement."

"Sorry, nothing to report. The only strange event was the case of the missing chisel. It seemed to have evaporated into thin air," Dad said with a shrug.

"What a coincidence! Grant found a chisel a couple of days ago near our second excavation site," Kenzie remarked. "Why would anyone involved in the renovation have a reason to be working around that area?"

"Anyway, it's gone now. I didn't see it when we returned for our lesson the next day," Grant added.

"Another Scottish mystery." Dad laughed.

"What about you, Mrs. Boyle? Do you have any new paintings that you care to share?" Kenzie asked.

"It's a work in progress," Mom said, returning with her partially completed rendering of the North Sea with its jagged picturesque rocks. Whimsical wildflowers of pink, yellow, and purple, interlaced with graceful windswept grasses, bordered the coastline, softening the primitiveness of the seascape's rugged terrain.

"Wow! Mrs. Boyle, this painting is magnificent," declared Kenzie. "If I wasn't so interested in photography, I think painting would be my next passion."

"Well, thank you, Kenzie. You're too kind," Mom replied with an appreciative smile.

"Anybody up for a game of croquet?" Charlie asked. "As I recall, I was the big winner the last time we played. Just wondering who's up for the challenge?" Charlie taunted, trying not to appear overly anxious to be alone with his coconspirators.

"You're on! Challenge accepted," Grant countered, pretending to throw down the gauntlet. The four teens retreated to the yard and began the masquerade. After what seemed like a fair amount of time, the group gathered around the patio table to brainstorm their next move. They decided that it would be impossible for them to sneak out in the middle of the night. So, the consensus was to meet at six o'clock the next morning to dig for the treasure. Riley's and Charlie's excuse was that they were meeting the twins for an early morning walk before Grant and Kenzie had class. With that settled, they went back to the game.

Down the street, not far away, the stranger listened intently to the what the four had planned.

Thanks for the heads up. Sorry to disappoint, but you're going to be in for a big surprise when you arrive at the cliffs tomorrow morning. The eavesdropper snickered.

Early the following morning, Grant and Kenzie arrived at the science building. They circled around back to the storage garage, where the excavation tools were housed. As Grant rounded the corner of the facility, he observed a figure entering the back door. Grant signaled for his sister to stop.

"What's up?" Kenzie asked, peering around her brother's shoulder to see what had caused him to hesitate.

"Somebody just went into the building. Don't you think it's a bit strange that someone would be here so early?" he whispered. "And I don't ever remember seeing that truck around here. Leaves one to wonder what's being concealed under that tarp. Maybe it has something to do with those disappearing invoices."

"OK, now my curiosity's got the best of me. Let's go over and check it out. You watch the door and signal me if you see any movement. This time I'll have my phone ready to take some pictures if necessary." The twins snuck over to the truck, picked up the tarp, and peered beneath it. They discovered a treasure trove of artifacts all nestled in protective crates. Grant snapped several pictures of the truck bed's historic contents.

"Let's get the shovels and scoot before the driver of this truck comes back," Kenzie pressed. Grant replaced the tarp, and then he and his sister headed to the garage opposite the truck to pick up the tools for the dig. The stranger emerged from the science building and caught a glimpse of the twins just as they were scurrying away.

"Now what in the world were those two up to? I certainly wasn't expecting them to be hanging around here," he muttered. "Whatever their agenda, it had better not involve snooping into my affairs." The mysterious individual walked over to the truck and began unloading the artifacts, all the while looking over his shoulder to make sure that no one was watching.

Riley and Charlie ran into the twins as they rushed out from between the buildings.

"Hey! What's the hurry?" asked Charlie. "If I didn't know better, I'd think that someone or something was chasing you." He laughed. "Please don't tell me there's a ghost connection to this place." Charlie's face now took on a more sober expression as he took the shovel from Grant.

"No ghosts, but we did stumble across someone entering the science building when we went to pick up the shovels," Grant explained.

"So, why would that cause you two to bolt? Maybe one of the instructors needed an early start to prep for class," Riley surmised.

"I agree. But the truck the person was driving hasn't been on campus before. At least I've never seen it," Grant responded. "Anyway, it piqued my curiosity, so Kenzie and I snooped under the truck's tarp and found that the bed contains several boxes of artifacts."

"Grant took pictures of the pieces so that this time we will have evidence if it comes to that," Kenzie said, interrupting. "Then we grabbed the shovels and got out of there."

"Well, I'd say that you've both had a rather nerve-racking morning," Riley responded. "It'll be interesting to research the items you photographed to see if any similar artifacts have been excavated in St. Andrews. But for now, I suggest that we make some history of our own and unearth that priceless thistle amulet. Fingers crossed that our experiment works." The four hiked off in the direction of the sandstone cliffs.

They certainly weren't prepared for the scene that played out before them. The euphoric excitement that once coursed through their entire bodies vanished, leaving the teens bewildered and dumbfounded. Two of the twelve painted areas designated for their excavation had already been disturbed. Riley was the first to break the silence as the group walked over to the gaping holes.

"How could this happen?" she asked, kneeling down next to one of the pits. "Someone seems to know our every move, but how?" She looked to the others for some sort of explanation.

"I wonder why whoever it was didn't dig up the rest of the plots?" Kenzie questioned. "Maybe whoever it was ran out of time and plans to return later."

"I think that I have the answer to your question, Kenzie," Grant replied as he sifted some of the loose dirt from the other hole and held out his hand. The three knelt next to Grant to see what he was holding. There in the middle of his palm were two stones—one a purple amethyst, the other a green emerald. No one spoke for a few seconds, trying to absorb what this meant.

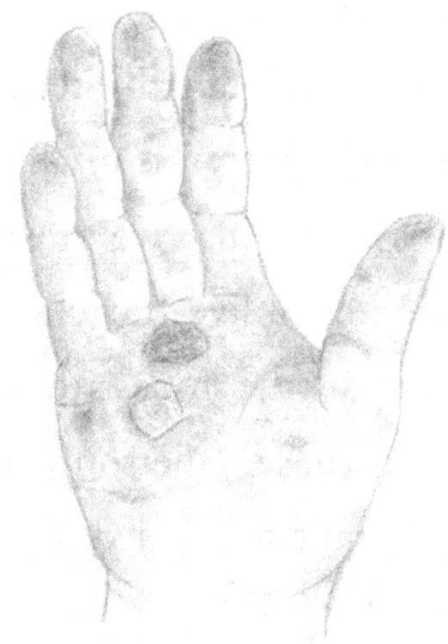

There in the middle of his hand were two stones-
one a purple amethyst, the other a green emerald.

"So, this means that the amulet was here!" Riley exclaimed. "The good news is that our experiment worked. The bad news is that someone else has this rare antique in his or her hands. This narrows it down to a few people. It must be someone who works either at the school or at the museum. Those are the only people we have spoken to about the amulet. Grant, if you transfer the pictures you took this morning to my phone, Charlie and I can go to the museum and check out the exhibits while you and Kenzie are in class. We can meet at the cottage when you're free and decide what to do next." Renewed determination resonated in Riley's voice.

Before the team went their separate ways, Grant gave Riley the precious stones for safekeeping.

"I figure the thief has already noticed that the stones are missing. He or she will undoubtedly return to the cliffs to look for them. When that person is unable to find them, he or she will logically assume that we are now in possession of the jewels. Kenzie and I live too close to the potential criminal. The farther away the stones are from the university, the better. It's less likely that the person will try to break into your family's rental," Grant concluded. Everyone agreed that Grant's suggestion made sense.

"Now it's off to the showers! Remember that we were supposed to be meeting the twins for a morning walk. We should appear to have worked up a sweat." He laughed, jogging in place.

"You go, Charlie," Kenzie teased.

Who'd have thought that a morning starting out with such high expectations would turn into a mixed bag of emotions—excitement, disappointment, hope, confusion, and lying just beneath the surface, apprehension?

Chapter Thirteen

Accident or Sabotage?

Mom greeted the teens as they walked into the kitchen. "So, how was your *very* early morning walk with the twins?" she asked, sounding a bit skeptical, knowing that her daughter and nephew weren't exactly early risers.

"Very energizing, Aunt Eleanor," Charlie remarked, pretending to stretch out his muscles to add credence to their fabricated narrative.

"By the way you're stretching, one would believe that you just had competed a twenty-five K." Mom laughed.

"I can see drama club in your future, Coz," Riley joked.

The cousins headed upstairs, showered, and then joined Riley's parents for breakfast.

While they were eating, Mom shared a pamphlet advertising sailing excursions on the *May Princess* to the Isle of May.

"The island lies five miles off the Fife coast and is an important national nature reserve. It's home to an amazing array of wildlife—up to two hundred thousand seabirds, including ninety thousand puffins, and about three hundred seals. Porpoise and dolphin and an occasional whale can be seen! You just must be on the trip on the right day, then you'll see these creatures if you're lucky. The trip on the boat lasts around five hours total. So, what do you think? Is anyone interested? If you'd like, we could invite Grant and Kenzie to join us. You girls might want to bring your cameras. I'm sure that you'd get some extraordinary pictures," Mom said.

"I can find time in my schedule," Dad answered. "Just let me know the day."

"Sounds terrific, Mom," Riley replied. "We'll check with the twins and try to coordinate a time."

Shortly after breakfast, the teens departed for the museum. Upon arriving, they made a beeline for the archaeological wing. Riley pulled up the photos on her phone that Grant had taken earlier that morning. The museum housed several exhibits of excavated antiquities.

"This is going to take all morning," Charlie complained. The cousins began their search for artifacts that were like the pictures on Riley's phone. After about an hour, they had reached the last few remaining displays.

"I guess this was a long shot." Riley sighed. "Maybe the pictures we have are the first of their kind for a new exhibit.

Let's look at the handful of exhibits at the end of this hall. Then we'll know that we've covered all our bases." Riley came to an abrupt halt when they reached the final showcase. She held the phone up next to the exhibit.

"Look, Charlie, it's a match!" Riley declared, trying to keep her voice in check. The display held pieces of grooved-ware pottery; tools fashioned from flint, possibly used for stripping bark and skinning animals; and two polished fifty-five-hundred-year-old stone balls. A stone towie ball decorated with intricate spiral patterns completed the collection.

"What seems to have the two of you so intrigued?" asked a woman's voice directly from behind them. Charlie and Riley turned and came face-to-face with Ms. Macpherson.

"We were commenting on how innovative people were in the past," Riley answered. "And just look at this towie ball. It's hard to imagine the time and patience it must have taken to carve these elaborate designs into a piece of stone." She was hoping that her explanation would suffice. "Do you know where these artifacts came from? Were they donated, or did the museum purchase them?" Riley was itching to see if they could get a handle on who owned the relics in the photos on her phone.

"I don't have that information off the top of my head. But if it doesn't have a sign stating that the exhibit was donated, then I assume it was purchased from someone selling on the private market. And, as I explained before, many private collectors have an intermediary, making these transactions secret. With all these questions, one would think that the two of you are studying to become curators," Macpherson concluded with a touch of sarcasm.

"No, we haven't declared majors yet." Charlie laughed. "We still have another year to figure out our course of study. Our friends, on the other hand, are totally committed to archaeology, so we kind of caught the fever. And speaking of our archaeological companions, we really should get going if we're going to connect with them on time."

"Good call, Charlie. It was nice seeing you again, Ms. Macpherson. Have a great day," Riley said with a smile.

As soon as the cousins were out of sight, Macpherson headed straight to her office to make an urgent call to Barclay.

"Great! Voicemail," she snapped. *I really need to get in touch with him. He needs to know that these teens think that they're on to something regarding the relics. And I don't think that they'll be easily dissuaded. It was a stroke of luck I happened to catch a glimpse of the picture on Riley's phone. I'm positive that the image was of an artifact that was listed on the invoice of items arriving with the next shipment. This entire scheme could blow up in our faces.* She was afraid, her hand trembling as she redialed the phone.

Meanwhile, Riley and Charlie had returned home just as Grant and Kenzie were coming up the walk. The usual pleasantries were exchanged as they headed outside. Mom and Dad were still out, so the foursome didn't have to put on the facade of playing croquet. They gathered at what they now jokingly called their "office of collusions and schemes."

"Here's what we found out about the pictures," Riley said, barely able to sit still. "We found some of the exact relics in one of the exhibits."

"In fact, it was in the very last showcase," Charlie interrupted.

"Anyway, guess who happened to come up behind us as we were comparing the pictures to the display? Ms. Macpherson. I'm not sure if she got a good look at my phone, but she did answer our question as to whether the items in the exhibit were donated or purchased. Although she didn't have the actual information at hand, she suggested that the items probably had been bought from a private collector through an intermediary. So, we need to investigate the ownership of the artifacts that were hidden in the truck," Riley concluded.

"Anybody have any bright ideas on how we're going to go about getting that particular bit of information?" Charlie quipped. "Hello, is there a Mr. Sherlock Holmes in the house perchance?" Charlie looked around as if expecting the elusive Holmes to appear.

"Grant and I are in and out of the science building all the time. We can snoop around when the lab isn't in use. When we returned from our session, we noticed that the truck containing the relics was gone. We're assuming that the artifacts we saw in the truck must be hidden somewhere on the premises, waiting for either payment or transport. And hopefully we'll come across some additional clues relating to the whereabouts and the person who took the amulet," Kenzie stated.

"Great idea, Ms. Holmes," Charlie extolled, giving Kenzie an approving smile. "So, what's the timeline for this next venture?"

"Well, we're busy tomorrow. Colin's taking us to an actual excavation site. We'll be working with other archaeologists. The weekend's out because we'd have no reason to be in the lab. So, how about Monday? Class has been canceled because of a rescheduled meeting, so we have some free time," Grant suggested.

"That'll work. Hey, how would the two of you like to go on an excursion to the Isle of May? My parents shared some info about the trip, and it sounds like it would be worth doing. Mom said that we could invite the two of you. Oh, and Kenzie, bring your camera. The animal life on the island will be incredible to photograph. I said that we'd check with you to see when you're free," Riley said.

"Our calendar is free this weekend. Just let us know what day your parents choose, and we'll be there. We've heard about the trip but haven't had the time to make it work. At this point, Kenzie and I are looking forward to spending a day on the water instead of toiling in the soil," Grant remarked, giving Riley a wink, a gesture that didn't go unnoticed by her cousin.

When opportunity knocks, you answer the door! the conspirator thought, almost giddy over the revelation of the upcoming excursion. *It's crucial that these four pests realize that this is no longer a game. In order to be shocked into reality, they need to experience what they believe to be a terrifying threat to their lives.*

Pieces of a plan began swirling around in his devious mind. Within a few minutes, those random thoughts came together in a concrete blueprint for how he would rid himself of the four interfering delinquents. *This ordeal will surely make an impact on their meddlesome behavior. First things first. The teens must realize that the accident they're about to experience is a result of their nosing around.* With that last thought, the conspirator set his crazed plan into motion.

Mom and Dad arrived home shortly after the members of the Collusions and Scheme Club had concluded their meeting. After checking the weather, everyone agreed that Saturday was the most favorable day for the excursion. Grant and Kenzie were to meet at the cottage. From there the group would take the bus down to the boat. Mom gave Grant one of brochures so he and Kenzie could read up on the trip at their leisure. When Grant put the pamphlet in his backpack, he noticed that he had left his textbook back at the science lab.

"Great! It looks like I left my book at school, and I have some reading to catch up on before tomorrow's dig," Grant said, getting up from the table. "Kenzie and I will be back early on Saturday."

"Thanks again for the invitation, Mr. and Mrs. Boyle," Kenzie said as they turned to leave.

* * *

Kenzie found Grant's textbook on one of the chairs in the lab. Picking up the book, she noticed a slip of paper sticking out from between two of the pages.

"What's this?" she asked her brother, handing him the manual. Grant took the book from his sister and pulled the foreign sheet out from between the pages. Kenzie could tell by the concerned look on her brother's face that this wasn't a love note. He held up the message for her to read:

JUST REMEMBER THIS NOTE! I TRIED TO WARN YOU! WHAT HAPPENS NEXT IS ON YOU!

"Do you think that this is some kind of sick joke?" Kenzie asked her brother, not sure if they should take this seriously.

"I really don't know. We received that other threatening note, and nothing happened. The only person who might be onto what we've been investigating is Ms. Macpherson. It's hard to believe that she'd be writing these ominous warnings. Although she does have a connection with Barclay, and he's in and out of here on any given day. I'll put this note away for safekeeping. Let's just continue with what we've been doing. I'll show Riley and Charlie the paper on Saturday and see what they think. For now, we'll take precautions by being aware of our surroundings," Grant reassured his sister.

Later that afternoon, Macpherson finally got hold of Barclay and shared the news of her earlier encounter with Riley and Charlie.

"So, with the photos they took, they now have proof that the artifacts are being brought in through the archaeological department. If they find out that these relics were excavated in Scotland, we're going to have a major problem on our hands. The Crown isn't a forgiving body when being cheated out of its rightful artifacts," Macpherson concluded in a tone that suggested she was in full meltdown mode.

"Slow down and take a breath, Barbara. I know it seems a bit dicey, but I have everything under control. Just let me handle the problem," Barclay cajoled his accomplice.

It was a beautiful crisp sunny morning when Riley's family, accompanied by the twins, left for the excursion. The experienced skipper and crew greeted each passenger with a hardy welcome as they stepped onto the deck. There were several seating options. The family chose to sit outside on the second level, where they'd have an excellent view. After everyone was on board, the boat left the small inlet and headed out to open waters. It wasn't exactly a smooth crossing. Huge plumes of water splashed against the bow of the sturdy boat as it cut through the rough sea.

After an hour's ride, the *Princess May* pulled in and docked. As passengers were disembarking, a ranger stationed on the Isle of May greeted them on the pier and gave a short talk on the latest information concerning the wildlife. He warned them to either wear a hat or hold a stick or an umbrella over their heads as they walked up the path. He explained that during this time of year, young birds were hatching. The adults are very protective and would dive-bomb, attacking people's heads. He also informed the visitors that there would be rangers on patrol during their stay on the island to answer any questions.

With sticks held high above their heads, Riley's troupe walked up the path unscathed. They were amazed to see thousands of birds soaring above their heads, with others huddled together nesting on the rocks. The high-pitched cacophony of sound made by the communicative gulls reverberated throughout the island. Snow-white wildflowers, ruffled by the breeze, blanketed the landscape. Large paunchy gray seals could be seen basking in the sun on the rocks below. While Riley and Kenzie were photographing the wildlife, Mom was making some quick sketches of the seascape. Dad, Grant, and Charlie opted for a more vigorous way to spend their time by hiking up some of the steeper cliffs.

After almost three hours onshore, a blast from the boat signaled that it was time to leave. With everyone accounted for, the transport departed. The winds were stronger now, causing turbulent seas. Choppy waves feverishly lashed at the boat, rocking it from side to side. The bow would rise vertically, pause, then crash back down into the angry surf. Taking every precaution, passengers were instructed to don life vests. The boat was about one mile offshore when it started taking on water.

The boat was about one mile offshore when it started taking on water.

The skipper sent out a mayday alarm requesting immediate assistance, while the crew searched every nook and cranny, trying to find the source of the breech.

"OK, I've had enough fun on the water," Grant complained, looking over at Riley while hanging onto the rail with an iron grip. Riley glanced back and gave him a half-hearted smile.

The death grip Kenzie had on Charlie's hand was turning his fingers white.

This would be a good time for a corny joke, Charlie thought. *Come on, think of something clever. Nope! I've got nothing. And I'm losing feeling in my hand.*

"You kids doing OK?" Dad shouted over the noise. "We're getting close to shore. Look over there, to your right." A coast guard rescue craft was speeding toward them. Once the boat was tied alongside the vessel, the sailors helped the passengers to disembark and board the rescue craft. The last leg of the ride was uneventful, much to the relief of the family and the other passengers.

"Who's up for some hot chocolate?" Mom asked once they were back on dry land. All hands went up. Later that evening, while listening to the radio, they found out that that the *Princess May* had taken on water because of a loose speedometer pickup hose. The skipper of the boat had been questioned about the mishap and had reassured the authorities that a complete inspection had been done the night before the cruise and that everything had checked out. He wasn't sure how the hose could have come loose. The final analysis was that it must have been a fluke, maybe caused by the boat slamming repeatedly into the surf.

While Mom and Dad were going about their business, the four teens headed outside for some fresh air. Once Grant was sure they were out of earshot, he shared the note that was left inside his book.

"Do you think the note has any connection to the unexplained loose hose on the boat?" Grant asked, hoping they would think that his question was way off base.

"I guess it's possible," Riley stated. "But would someone go as far as to harm all those people on the cruise? I mean, a hundred people could have drowned, and for what? We know that someone found the amulet, so is this a ploy to keep us from finding out his or her identity? And then there's the question of the artifacts and the mysterious shipment. Is that worth killing for?"

"It's just that last statement written on the note, 'What happens next is on you.' It seems like the person threatening us was giving a forewarning of what had happened on the boat," Kenzie explained.

"I see your point, Kenzie, but if I thought that we were in danger, I'd tell my parents, and they'd notify the authorities. I think that we're letting our imaginations get the best of us. Let's continue to keep a low profile. Absolutely no more water excursions. And remember, if one of us gets into trouble, we have our secret weapon," Riley concluded, pointing to her cell phone.

"OK, so I guess that we're still on for Monday," Grant acknowledged. "Kenzie and I will look around the lab. Maybe there's a secret drawer or door that could lead us to a clue." He seemed hopeful.

This is unbelievable! After the trauma they experienced, they're still willing to pursue what they foolishly regard as their selfless mission in life. I'll have to wait until I can get one of them alone—ideally, one of the girls. One of them shouldn't put up much of a fight. I wonder what they consider to be their secret weapon. Anyway, I'm going to have to move quickly now that they're sniffing around the lab. If they find that hidden door and find what's in the secret room, the game's over, the hidden onlooker thought, feeling frantic.

Chapter Fourteen

Held Captive

At breakfast Monday morning, Dad was notified that the construction was on hold for inspection. The crew would have the day off, so there was no need for him to be on-site.

"Well, that works out nicely. I was trying to squeeze in some time for a trip to Edinburgh to pick up a few things for the renovation. Your mom's busy today, so who's up for a little road trip?" Dad asked the teens.

"We're supposed to meet the twins later this morning. Why don't you and Charlie go?" Riley suggested. "You can do some uncle and nephew bonding. I'll meet the twins, and Charlie can catch up with us when he returns."

"Sounds like a plan to me. What do you say, Uncle? It's you and me and the open road." Charlie laughed.

After everyone had left the house, Riley made her way to the North Campus, anxious to hear if the twins were able to steal some time away to search for any evidence on the whereabouts of the artifacts or amulet. She was a bit early, so she decided to check out her dad's project. She found an open door leading to the renovation.

Riley's arrival didn't go undetected by the individual peering out of the second-story window. He watched as she entered the worksite. *Wonder what she's doing here without her partner in crime*? he thought. *She certainly is a nosy one! Time to see what's piqued her insatiable curiosity.* He took the back stairs, hoping to remain unnoticed.

"I guess that the inspectors haven't arrived yet. Or they've been here and they've left," Riley surmised. It was difficult to see. The only illumination came from the roughed-in subterranean windows. When her eyes finally adjusted to the dim light, she was able to see how the reconstruction was progressing. The smell of fresh-cut lumber lingered, and the odor of damp, musty rock hung in the air. Riley made her way along the corridor until she came to a short hallway on her left.

I wonder where this leads, she thought as she felt her way along the wall. *It looks like the construction crew hasn't gotten to this part of the project.*

When she got to the end, her fingers came across what felt like some sort of lever. She pushed down on the trigger, and to her surprise, the stone wall opened. "Oh my gosh! A secret door," she cried. It was just wide enough for her to squeeze through. "OK, let's see what's in here." She turned her body sideways in order to shimmy through the narrow opening. As she was attempting to squeeze through the tight space, her rear pocket got snagged on something protruding from the door. In attempting to set herself free, she accidently jarred her phone from her pocket. It tumbled to the floor behind some discarded pieces of lumber.

Riley never heard the muffled footsteps as they approached the partially opened door. As she was steadying herself and attempting to get her bearings, she heard a scraping sound from out in the hallway. Before she could react, the door slammed shut. Suddenly, she found herself in total darkness! She ran to the door and pushed against it as hard as she could. The door wouldn't budge. She yelled for help. She pressed her head against the door, hoping that someone had heard her cries. Nothing. The only sound echoing in her ears was the pounding of her own heart and the frantic gasping for breath as she struggled for air. After several minutes, she was able to fight the panic that gripped her body like a vise. She got her breathing under control, and her heart stopped drumming in her ears.

"Slow down and think, girl," she whispered. *Maybe the inspectors haven't arrived yet. Plan A, I'll listen for their voices and then start yelling. Plan B, if that doesn't work, I'm sure that the twins will get worried when I don't show up to meet them. Plan C, just wait and remain calm,* she told herself.

The uninvited observer was still watching. *Let's see if this shakes up the annoying foursome, knowing that I can get to anyone of them. I'll leave her locked up long enough for her to reflect on the possible ominous consequences that they could suffer if they don't drop their detectives' club insufferable meddling.* He scoffed as he crept away.

Grant and Kenzie arrived at the science building a few minutes after Riley. If they had gotten there just a tad earlier, they might have seen Riley enter the construction site. While they waited for the cousins, they decided to explore the room. Kenzie kept watch while Grant began a methodical search of the lab. They were so engrossed in their quest to find a link to either the artifacts or the amulet that they lost track of time. When Grant finally took a break and checked his watch, he realized that Riley and Charlie were considerably late meeting them.

"What do you suppose happened to Riley and Charlie?" Grant questioned. "It's not like them to be late and not call. I'll try Riley's cell. Normally I wouldn't worry, but with those crazy threats and that bizarre accident on the boat the other day, I'm a bit leery when something happens out of the norm." He punched in Riley's number. It went straight to voicemail.

"Try Charlie's number. They're usually together. Maybe Riley forgot to charge her phone," Kenzie suggested. Grant tried Charlie's number.

"Straight to voicemail," Grant responded through clenched teeth. His furrowed brow showed the depth of his concern.

"Let's try the tracker," Kenzie prompted. "I don't think that we'd be invading their privacy. We'd feel terrible if something happened to them because we failed to act. I'm positive that if the shoe were on the other foot, Charlie and Riley would react the same way."

Grant turned on the tracker, which immediately started sending out a signal.

"Here we go. Riley is somewhere close by." The twins followed the signal, which led them to the renovation site. Colin was exiting as Grant and Kenzie approached the open door.

"Hi, Mr. Balfour. I thought that the staff was in meetings all day," Grant said.

"We're taking a short break. I thought that I'd sneak in and see how the construction was progressing. Looks like it should be completed in a few weeks. It'll be nice to be able to spread out. We certainly can use the added storage with the number of additional artifacts arriving almost daily. Time to head back. I don't want them starting without me. Be careful if you're going to walk around inside. It's difficult to see until your eyes adjust to the dimness. We don't want anything happening to my two budding archaeologist, now, do we?" he commented as he strode out the door.

"Is your tracker still picking up a signal from Riley's phone?" Kenzie asked as they walked deeper into the dimly lit room.

"Yeah, and it appears from the screen that she should be right down this hall." Grant yelled, "Riley, are you here somewhere? Can you hear me?" A small muffled sound came from the other side of the stone wall.

"I'm in here, behind the door," Riley answered, relieved that someone had finally come to her rescue. "There's a lever along the wall. Push it down and the door should open," she instructed. Grant found the latch and pushed it downward, which allowed the door to open slightly.

"Can you pull it open a little wider?" she urged. As Grant and Kenzie pulled on the door, Riley used the weight of her body to push against the stubborn obstacle standing between her and her friends. With the combined effort of the three of them, they were able to enlarge the entrance to the hidden room. Riley stepped out into the dimly lit hallway. She retrieved her phone from behind the pile of scrap lumber.

"Are you all right?" Kenzie asked, hugging her friend. "What happened? How in the world did you end up getting locked in that room?" Riley explained the events leading up to her being trapped inside the storage area.

"After I squeezed through the opening, I heard a scraping sound, and before I could move, the door shut behind me. I called out for help, but no one answered. It all happened so fast. I'm just thankful that you thought of using the tracker." She sighed, smiling up at Grant.

"We tried to contact Charlie, but the call went straight to voicemail," Grant explained.

"Charlie drove up to Edinburgh with my dad. He was going to catch up with us later when he got home. Maybe it's a good thing that he had his phone turned off. If he had taken your call, my dad would have found out that I was missing, and then our entire operation would have been torpedoed. So long as we're here, let's look to see if there are any clues as to what would have been stored in this hidden room," Riley proposed.

"Just make sure one of us remains outside to guard the door. That's all we'd need is the three of us locked up in this small room like a can of sardines," Grant teased.

The girls turned on their phone flashlights and crept inside. Although the shelves in the room were bare, there was a residue of sand and soil scattered across the wooden planks, as if the planks had once held objects dug from the earth.

"Do you think this is where the mysterious artifacts were stored after we saw them on the truck?" Kenzie asked. "This would be the perfect place to hide illegal relics until they're ready to be sold."

"Makes sense to me. And if this was used as storage for nefarious reasons, then where is the collection now? If I were to make an educated guess, I'd bet that the construction crew is about to work on this section next, so to play it safe, the merchandise had to be relocated. I'm not sure if this is getting us any closer to finding out who's behind this scheme," Riley concluded with obvious disappointment in her voice.

As the girls were about to leave, Riley happened to glance down. That's when she spotted an object on the floor in the corner under one of the shelves. She bent down and extracted the object from the shadows.

"What did you find?" Kenzie inquired, kneeling next to her friend to get a better look.

"It's a chisel. I wonder if this is the same one that went missing a few days ago? If so, what would someone be doing with it in here? And then there's the chisel that you found, Grant," she called out through the semiopen doorway. "One day it was at the site, and the next day it vanished. So, we can add one more mystery to our list." Riley sounded exasperated.

The girls emerged from the chamber with the chisel. Grant rotated the tool in his hand.

"This looks exactly like the one I found. I remember that the one I picked up had a small nick at the tip. I also know that this isn't even close to any type of equipment used in excavating. Colin assured me of that. So, let's look at the chisel puzzle pieces. We can assume that this instrument belongs to someone on the construction crew. So, can we also assume that this person was snooping around the cliffs and accidently dropped the tool? Then, after realizing it was missing, he recovered it and brought it back to the building?" Grant asked, hoping that his theory held an inkling of merit.

"It sounds feasible so far," Kenzie agreed. "Our next step is to figure out who would be using a chisel at this stage of the renovation. I thought they had removed the stone earlier so the carpenters could rough in the walls. Remember how we were all hoping that there might be something valuable hidden behind the thistle stone that had been removed then recemented?" There was excitement in her voice.

"That's it!" Riley blurted. "What if the person who either owns or stole the chisel used it to remove a stone, hide the amulet, and then recement the rock? There were several people in and out of the construction site when the rock with the thistle marking was about to be removed. I remember how everyone witnessing the stone's removal held their breath in anticipation, dying to see what secret the cavity was about to reveal. This could have inspired our thief to restage the scene in another location, probably off campus, where he knew no one would think to look." Grant and Kenzie both nodded, acknowledging the possibility.

"So, now all we need to do is find some rock somewhere in some remote place that looks as if it's been disturbed recently. Piece of cake." Grant laughed.

"Yeah, that could be somewhat of a problem," Riley agreed, her brows knitted together in thought. "But I think that the culprit's getting desperate, because he's transferring the antiquities from one place to another. It looks like he's trying to stay one step ahead of us. Here's my theory based on the following facts: First you discovered the artifacts in a strange vehicle. Second, the items disappeared from said vehicle. Third, they were stored in the hidden room until they had to be moved again, possibly because of the construction or because of us. You know what bothers me? I still can't figure out how this person is privy to all our plans. It's as if he planted a bug on all of us. But of course, that's impossible." Riley was frustrated at having no answers.

"Let's get out of the dungeon," Kenzie begged. "I think that we'll all feel better once we're out in the sun."

"Oh, by the way, Riley, did you happen to see Colin when you entered the building?" Grant inquired.

"No. I thought that you said there were meetings scheduled for today. So, why would Colin be down here?" Riley pressed, as the three teens walked out of the dimly lit structure.

"Kenzie and I ran into him when we were looking for you. He said that they were on a break, so he decided to see how the renovation was progressing. Do you think that Colin could have been the person responsible for locking you in the storage room?" Grant asked, finding it hard to believe that his instructor could do something so callous.

"I have no idea. It all happened so quickly. Like I said before, I heard a scraping sound, and before I could react, the door was pushed shut," Riley remarked with a shrug. "Let's head over to the cottage. Maybe Charlie's back and we can see what his take is on this latest disturbing incident."

Chapter Fifteen

Finally, Another Lead!

When the three teens arrived home, Dad and Charlie were just pulling up to the house. Mom greeted them at the door. Her strained expression telegraphed that something had happened to upset her. Dad was the first to inquire about the cause of her distress. Mom detailed the event that nearly sent her to the hospital.

"OK, remember I told you that I was going back to the Heritage Museum, you know, the one with the beautiful garden in the back? Anyway, while I was walking up the road, I dropped my pencil case. When I bent over to pick it up, an old ratty truck sped by, nearly hitting me. The driver never stopped or looked back to see if I was injured. That's highly uncharacteristic of the people in this town. Everyone I've met has been friendly and extremely courteous. I just couldn't believe that someone could be so irresponsible," she concluded. The tremor in her voice indicated that she was still trying to process what had happened.

"Oh my gosh, Mom, I'm so sorry that you had such a scare. We're just happy that you're OK," Riley said, giving her mom a comforting hug.

"I second that sentiment, Aunt Eleanor. Can you describe the truck?" Charlie asked, giving Riley and the twins a look that indicated this might get them closer to solving at least one of the mysteries.

Mom's description matched the vehicle Grant and Kenzie saw behind the science building.

"I'll keep a lookout for the truck. If I see the driver, I'm going to give him a piece of my mind!" Charlie declared.

"No, you're not!" Mom countered. "Just leave things be. I'm not hurt, just a bit shaken up. I'm going to make myself a cup of tea and relax." She turned and walked back into the house.

"Let's go out back and let Mom have some peace and quiet," Riley suggested, anxious to discuss this new morsel of information. The four left the house and headed for the croquet set. Teams were chosen, and the game began. Apparently, Charlie was a tad off his game. His first shot found itself lodged underneath the patio table. He wormed his way under the piece of furniture and reached for the ball. As he was withdrawing, he clunked his head on the table.

"Ouch!" he yelped. He raised his hand to rub his head. At that moment, his hand hit something attached to the underside of the table. A closer look revealed something that resembled a small speaker. He quickly took out his phone and snapped a picture. Then with the errant ball in his hand, he slowly inched his way back out from beneath the menacing table. He put his finger to his lips.

"OK, I've had enough of this game. I must have lost my touch. Who's up for a walk to the cafe on the quad? I could go for a cold drink," Charlie proposed, signaling for the others to follow.

Riley checked in with Mom to see how she was doing and to let her know they were off to the cafe. Once the foursome was far away from the house, Charlie shared the picture of what he had found under the table.

"OK, so this solves the mystery of how this crazed individual has always been aware of our next move," Riley reasoned. "We can use this to our advantage. Our next conversation should be about dropping our investigation. Let him or her think that we've exhausted all our leads and that there's no path forward. That way he or she will let down his or her guard and feel free to move ahead with whatever scheme is on the agenda. All we need is one careless mistake." Riley gave everyone a high five.

"Now that we have addressed how we're going to handle our unwelcome eavesdropper, what's our next move regarding the truck that nearly struck your mom?" Kenzie asked. Several ideas were batted around. The group decided that a trip to the museum was the next logical move.

"Riley and I can check out the museum while the two of you are in class. It's not very large, so it shouldn't take too long to scope out the place," Charlie remarked. "Maybe the culprit hid the artifacts somewhere among the other antique pieces. You know, like camouflage. So, we need to examine each exhibit for relics like the ones in the pictures. I think that we're finally onto something." He was itching to start the quest for the antiquities.

"Sounds like a plan, Charlie," Riley added. "But first, let's head back to the cottage and lay the trap for this uninvited intruder." The foursome practiced the conversation they were about to have for the eavesdropper's benefit. When they arrived at the house, they set their plan in motion. Following their cameo performances, it was time for another competitive game of croquet.

"Are you sure that you're up for this, Charlie?" teased Kenzie. "The last time you struck the ball, your sense of direction was just a tad off." She handed him the mallet.

"A tad off? You're being too kind. It was like he was swinging for the fences." Grant chuckled, taking a baseball stance and holding his mallet like a baseball bat.

"OK. OK, very funny, guys. So, I powered up a bit too much. I guess that I don't know my own strength," Charlie said, hitting his ball through the first wicket.

How in the world did that girl escape being locked in the hidden room? I can't imagine how anyone could even find that chamber, let alone find the girl. I guess her escaping on her own or with help saved me the problem of figuring out how to release her without exposing my identity. Whatever. It appears that they have finally gotten the message. It's about time! Now I can finalize the sale of this latest shipment of artifacts with the museum. The amulet is hidden off campus in the countermine tunnel, so there's no way anyone can connect me with the antique treasure. And from what I've overheard, Riley's father should be completing his architectural responsibilities, which means the family will soon be taking their leave. Good riddance! I'll retrieve the amulet after their departure, the intruder thought, satisfied with the way things were finally falling into place.

Chapter Sixteen

Perplexing Curiosities

The following morning, Grant and Kenzie were in the lab gathering their equipment when they heard Colin calling out for one of them to please grab the paperwork for today's project. The packet was on the desk in the office. Grant finished packing his tools, then went in search of the required documents. This time the paperwork was right where Colin had said it would be, no searching necessary. As Grant turned to leave, he noticed a sheet of paper on the floor next to the shredder.

Not sure if this sheet missed being shredded or if it accidently fell off the desk, he thought as he bent down to retrieve the misplaced document. *Well now, what do we have here?* Finding himself staring at an unusual rendition of what appeared to be a map, he took a picture of the drawing with his phone, placed the paper back on the floor next to the shredder, then left to join his sister.

"Wait until I show you what I found on the office floor," Grant whispered. "I'll show you the picture later when we catch up with Riley and Charlie. It might mean nothing, but I don't want to take a chance if this is a clue."

"Gotcha," Kenzie said. They headed out to the truck.

Meanwhile, Charlie and Riley had arrived at the Heritage Museum and were ready to begin their investigation.

"We're kind of like archaeologists," Charlie stated. "You know, searching for artifacts. The only difference is that the relics that we're looking for are already dug up. And look, no dirt: our hands are clean." He rubbed his hands together then held them up for his cousin to see.

"Quiet! We don't want anyone to know the real reason we're here," Riley whispered, shaking her head and rolling her eyes at her cousin. They began their hunt for what could possibly be illegally obtained museum pieces. The old wooden floors creaked as they walked from room to room. Charlie entered a small alcove that displayed pharmaceuticals. The exhibit contained drugs, medical tools, old bottles, and medical books, but nothing that resembled the items in the picture. Riley's examination of the dentistry exhibited revealed carved teeth made by the local jeweler. It was interesting, but not what she was hoping to find. Charlie's and Riley's paths converged in the last room, which housed several scales and replicas of items that one might find in grocery store.

"Now what?" Charlie asked, looking around for another room to explore.

"Let's take a walk to the gardens out back," Riley suggested. "If the careless driver who almost hit my mom was transporting something illegal, maybe he hid it somewhere out of sight in the back of the museum."

The two followed a brick path out into the picturesque garden. As they continued, they came across a small building with a green door. Charlie turned the latch and pushed open the door. The cousins found themselves in an old and dusty wooden room. Three sides of the room contained shelving. There was a door and a small window on the back wall, which let in enough light to allow for an adequate search of the room. The two detectives went to work checking each box. Footsteps outside the window startled the two, causing them to drop to their knees out of sight below the glass.

"That was close," whispered Charlie. "We'd better get a move on. See anything that looks out of place?"

"No. Most of the boxes look like they've been here forever," Riley answered, wiping her dusty hands on her jeans.

"I've got two more boxes, then that's it," Charlie announced. As he moved the last box, he noticed a small door behind the shelf. "Hey, Riley! Come over and check this out." He began removing the remaining boxes from the shelf. When the shelving was clear, he pulled the unit away from the wall and open the panel. There, right inside the opening, was a box. Charlie extracted the package from the obscure storage cavity.

"OK, let's see what's inside," Charlie said. He lifted the cardboard lid and very carefully began pulling away the straw packing. The contents in the box revealed the artifacts that were depicted in the photos.

"Well, I guess we've found the missing relics," Riley declared. "So, now that we found them, what should we do with them?" She looked up at her cousin for advice.

"Let me take a minute to think," he said, running his hand through his hair.

"It had better be a quick minute. If we stay here much longer, someone is bound to find us," Riley challenged. She began repacking the box.

"I think that we put everything back the way we found it. We really don't have any proof that something unlawful is transpiring. We need to do more investigating to find out who owns the box," Charlie concluded. The cousins had just set the room back in order when the door suddenly opened, causing Riley and Charlie to nearly jump out of their skin.

"What are you doing in here?" the curator asked, not trying to hide his displeasure.

Trying to appear as calm as possible while shaking on the inside, Riley said, "Ah, well, you see, we were visiting your unique museum. By the way, I found it quite interesting to learn that the local jeweler, not a dentist, designed the teeth.

Anyway, back to why we're here. My mom visited a few days ago and had told us about the garden and how rustic it is and how beautifully it is designed. So, after we toured your museum, we wandered outside to see the gardens for ourselves. We thought this building was part of the tour, so we let ourselves in. I hope that's OK.

"Would you have time to explain who worked here and what he did?" Riley pleaded, hoping this would get them a reprieve.

Satisfied with Riley's excuse, the curator was happy to oblige.

"This building housed the local blacksmith. He was responsible for forging and sharpening tools. These exhibits showcase some of the hardware used in the execution of the job." The curator explained each tool and its purpose.

When his presentation ended, he escorted the cousins from the building. On the way back through the museum, Riley asked the curator if the museum ever exhibited archaeological artifacts. Their host explained that if they had an interest in that subject matter, they should visit St. Andrews Museum, which housed several interesting exhibits.

"I just have one more question," Riley interjected. "Would you possibly know the identity of the person who drives an old gray pickup truck? It seems that his quick reaction saved my mother from serious injuries, and we'd like to thank him. Mom didn't have the opportunity to express her gratitude because the driver was well on his way by the time she pulled herself together."

"You mean the driver didn't stop to see if you mother was OK?" the curator asked, sounding horrified that someone could be so inconsiderate.

"Mom said that whoever was driving the truck was in a hurry. The driver probably checked her out in the rearview mirror, saw that she wasn't injured, and continued to his destination," Riley answered, quite pleased with her explanation.

"The truck is a community vehicle. It's shared among several of the museums and the university. It's normally housed at the St. Andrews Museum. That way, when someone needs a truck, they borrow it and then return it to St. Andrews," explained the curator. Riley and Charlie thanked the gentleman and quickly took their exit.

Sitting in an old gray pickup truck parked behind the garden building, the onlooker watched the scene play out between the curator and the teens. His senses were on high alert. Up until now, he felt that he had everything under control.

I thought those two had given up on being amateur detectives. So, why are they snooping around here? he questioned. *It could be that their visit is totally innocent. Maybe I'm overreacting because we're so close to finalizing the transaction. Nothing or no one must sabotage this acquisition!*

"This latest information about who may have driven the truck broadens the playing field," Riley stated as she and Charlie made their way over to the university to meet the twins. "I mean, it could be any number of people working at the school or at one of the other museums. Let's revisit what we do know. Ms. Macpherson and Barclay both have connections to the museum in Edinburgh. They resumed their relationship when Macpherson took over the curatorship in St. Andrews. After the heated argument I overheard, we know the involvement between the two isn't casual. My gut feeling is that they're working with someone either at the university or at one of the other museums. What's your opinion, Sherlock?"

"I agree that they're our two prime suspects. It's just hard to imagine either of them writing threatening notes and locking you in a room, let alone sabotaging a boat carrying a hundred passengers," Charlie answered. "I say that we run our theory by Grant and Kenzie and get their take on who they think might be capable of committing such heinous acts." Charlie signaled to his cousin that the twins were just up ahead. The four exchanged greetings, then took a seat under a nearby tree, distancing themselves from potential eavesdroppers.

"Well, we sure had a productive morning!" Riley declared. She related the events leading up to the discovery of the missing artifacts and the precarious situation they were in when the curator pushed open the door and encountered them standing in the middle of the room.

"He was none too happy," Charlie added. "But we did find out about who owns the gray truck." After sharing all the remaining details, Riley posed the question.

"So, what do you think we should do about the artifacts, and whom do the two of you suspect?" Riley asked, the tone in her voice reflecting her exasperation.

"Wonderful! Now we're back trying to solve two mysteries," Kenzie moaned. "Wait until you see what Grant has on his phone. You're on, Grant." She gave a wave of her hand as if introducing a celebrity.

Grant was eager to share the picture he had taken of the map earlier that morning.

"What do you think, guys? It sure looks like a map to me," Grant stated as he passed his phone to the others to get their opinion. Charlie and Kenzie had their heads together, trying to make out the meaning of the symbols and measurements in the drawing.

"Let's start with the marking on the rock," Kenzie recommended. "It might indicate that a piece of rock had been chiseled from the stone, possibly marking where the amulet was hidden." She held up the phone for the others to see. "Its appearance would be insignificant to anyone passing by. It would look as if the stone had been chipped. Then there's this rectangle. Not sure what that's supposed to represent. The numbers and arrows on the bottom of the page could indicate feet or yards. The arrows run from the beginning of the passageway and stop at the stone. What are the possibilities that this is a map leading to a hidden object buried behind the chipped rock?"

"Oh my gosh!" Grant said, interrupting. "Riley, this could be the scenario that you proposed a few days ago. It could be some rock somewhere that has recently been disturbed, a cavity behind a rock large enough to hide—"

"The amulet!" Riley cried out, cutting Grant off midsentence. "Whoa. But there are so many buildings in St. Andrews constructed with stone. Where do we start? Does anything in this drawing resemble a place that looks familiar to either of you?" Riley was hoping against hope that something in the photo would trigger a positive response.

"Like you said, Riley, all the buildings look the same. It's as if stone was the only building material used hundreds of years ago. This is overwhelming. I suggest that we let the picture ruminate in our minds. Kind of toss it around, mull it over. The same thing goes with the artifacts," Grant offered.

"Jeez! With all this ruminating, we sound like cows," joked Charlie, laughing at his own wisecrack. "All kidding aside, Grant, that's good advice. Right now, my brain is scrambled. So, now that we're just hanging around ruminating with nothing to do, does anyone have an idea for a field trip?"

After some thought, Kenzie proposed they go to the castle and explore the countermine.

"It's really a unique experience. Let me give you the CliffsNotes version.

"Hold on, Kenzie. I have one rather important question. Are ghosts included in this totally unique experience? 'Cause it seems like every interesting site comes with its own peculiar brand of apparition," Charlie said, feeling leery about what they might encounter in the mine.

"Not to worry," Kenzie remarked, giving Charlie a reassuring pat on the shoulder. "To my knowledge, there are no ghosts. Hmm, although with what I'm about to tell you, you'd think there would be a least one unhappy spook haunting the mine. I am a bit of an expert on the mine! Anyway, here's the history of the mines.

"In the 1540s, the church was under threat from a growing number of reformers. They were unhappy with the clergy, who enjoyed lavish lifestyles despite their vows of poverty.

"In 1546, in front of the castle walls, the Protestant preacher George Wishart was burned for heresy, ordered by Cardinal Beaton, who hoped to counter the religious and political threat to his authority. Between five and six o'clock on the morning of May twenty-ninth, a group of men set off toward the castle. Workmen were busy around the castle walls, and the drawbridge had been lowered to allow entrance. The conspirators disguised themselves as masons and entered the castle grounds unnoticed. The alarm was eventually raised. The workmen and the guards fled, and the castle was taken. Cardinal Beaton realized his castle had been overrun. The conspirators killed Beaton.

"After Beaton's murder, the earl ordered the conspirators to be removed from the castle. Toward the end of 1546, trying to hasten the end of the battle, the Earl of Arran tried to break through the defenses by digging a mine beneath the tower gate. They hoped to bring down the walls by igniting gunpowder under the foundations. The earl's plan was foiled by those in the castle, who responded by digging a countermine to intercept that of the earl. After two unsuccessful attempts, a third mine was excavated, but it was off course. Eventually the conspirators were dispelled," Kenzie concluded. "See, no mention of ghosts." She laughed.

"That's quite a story," Riley declared. "I bet my dad would be interested in seeing how the countermine is constructed."

"It sounds like something worth exploring," Charlie acknowledged.

"You know, before we head off to the mine, what do you think about going to the library and making two enlarged copies of the map? Having the actual drawing in hand might make it easier to compare it to possible sites that may be concealing the amulet," Riley suggested.

With everyone in agreement, the foursome set off for the library.

Chapter Seventeen

An Ill-Fated Conversation

Upon entering the library, the teens found an isolated computer far away from prying eyes. They downloaded the photo from Grant's phone, then proceeded to make two copies of the map. With that task addressed, the group made their way to St. Andrews Castle.

With that task addressed, the group made their way to St. Andrews Castle.

"Oh dear, I forgot to ask if either of you is claustrophobic," Kenzie said apologetically.

"We're good," Charlie replied, giving his tour guide an approving smile and a thumbs-up.

"OK, guys, before we start down into the mine, here's a heads-up on what to expect," Grant cautioned. "It's very narrow, dimly lit, slippery, and damp, and hopefully you have strong backs, because you'll be bent over most of the time as you inch your way through the mine. There are lights spaced throughout the cavern, along with a handrail to help guide you along.

"Not exactly a tour highlighted in a magazine targeting the lifestyles of the rich and famous," Charlie teased. "At least we won't be on a sinking excursion ship in the middle of the North Sea, so that's a plus."

The four followed in single file, with Grant leading the way. Grant was right: the chiseled stone stairs descending into the mine were narrow and a bit slippery. The hunched-over teens treaded slowly and carefully through the mine's constricted passage, stopping occasionally to remark about some aspect of the tunnel that caught their attention.

They were about halfway through their tour when Riley slipped and lost her balance. She reached out and caught hold of the wall to steady herself. In doing so, her hand raked across a jagged stone, causing a substantial cut.

"Ouch! That hurt!" Riley cried out. As she pulled her hand away from the rock, she noticed the stone appeared to have a small nick, leaving rough edges where it had been chipped away. Riley could feel the blood trickling down her hand and arm. Luckily, they were near one of the lights, allowing them to assess the damage.

"It doesn't look too bad. But we need to stop the bleeding. We can use this," Grant said, carefully wrapping Riley's hand in his handkerchief. "Let's get you home. This gash needs to be washed, disinfected, and then a bandaged in a clean dressing."

"Yes, Doc," Riley agreed, eager to get back to the cottage and tend to her throbbing hand.

Mom was out when the four arrived home. Dad greeted them when they walked into the great room.

"What happened to you, sweetie?" Dad asked, seeing the bloody cloth wrapped around his daughter's hand. Riley explained how the accident had happened as Dad tended to her hand. Riley noticed that she had some bloodstains on her jeans, so she excused herself and went upstairs to change. She made sure to remove the map from her pocket so it wouldn't get ruined in the wash. She set the map on the bed and went back down to rejoin the others. The four teens got some cold drinks from the refrigerator and wandered outside. Knowing that their conversations were being monitored, they kept their chatter focused on what courses they would be enrolled in for the fall semester.

Upon returning home, Mom set down her supplies, waved a quick hello to her husband, then headed upstairs to gather the laundry. They'd be leaving in a few days, and she wanted to get ahead of the dirty clothes before they had to pack. She grabbed Charlie's clothes and proceeded to Riley's hamper.

Surprised to see the stains on her daughter's jeans, she started out the door when she saw a drawing resembling a map on the bed.

Now I have two questions, she thought. *First and foremost, what happened to my daughter? And why does she have this map? These two had better not be related, Miss Boyle!* Dad explained Riley's run-in with the wall to his wife and reassured her that the gash had been disinfected and a clean dressing had been applied.

"Did our daughter say anything about a map?" Mom inquired, showing her husband the paper in her hand.

"No. We were focused on cleaning and bandaging her hand. I don't think this paper had anything to do with the accident," Dad answered nonchalantly.

"Well, I have some questions. You know our daughter. If there's a mystery, she'll be involved somewhere, somehow." With that statement, she headed outside to confront her detective offspring. Mom acknowledged the teenagers as she came into the yard.

"OK, my darling daughter, how is your hand? Dad told me about the hand mishap. Do you need anything for the pain?" Mom asked, putting her arm around Riley's shoulder. Riley couldn't help but notice the paper in her mother's hand.

"You know, Mom, it does kind of throb. I think I'll just run in and get something from the medicine chest," Riley said, getting up from the table, eager to leave before her mom had a chance to ask about the map. "I'm sure that Charlie, Grant, or Kenzie would love to tell you about the countermine."

"Wait a minute, young lady. When I was collecting dirty clothes, I found this on your bed. We only have a few days left in St. Andrews, and so far, we've had no unfortunate mishaps. And now I find what, a treasure map? And what treasure do you hope to find behind some stones?" Mom asked, her voice taking on a serious tone.

"I found the map, Mrs. Boyle," Grant offered. "I thought it would be a hoot if we attempted to find out where it might lead. But judging from the clues, I think it would be like looking for a certain stone in a city of stone." He shrugged.

"I agree with you. It really doesn't look very promising," Mom said. Then she followed Riley into the house.

So much for waiting until the family leaves. I'm going to have to step up my game plan. Good ole Mom has a right to be concerned. Just don't get in my way, dear children. I'm beginning to think that the amulet is cursed. First, Lars fell to his death when it was in his possession. And now because those nosy amateur detectives are determined to find it, their sleuthing landed them smack in the middle of my lucrative transactions with the museum. Moving ahead with the sale is essential to obtaining funds necessary to subsidize my project. I need to move immediately. At least I don't have to worry about them finding the amulet. The map is so obscure that they'll never figure out where that national treasure is hidden. He sneered. *Time to make a call to my intermediary. He can pick up the merchandise at the post office tomorrow and complete the sale.*

Riley came downstairs just in time to say goodbye to the twins. The cousins followed Grant and Kenzie down the walk.

"Great recovery, Grant," Riley praised. "Everything you said was the truth. No sense getting Mom upset over something that will probably never materialize. You know, I've been thinking. We seem to be stuck with no way forward. We can't go to the police about the artifacts because we have no evidence. If we tell my parents, well, you know what they'll say. So, what if we speak to Professor Abernathy? He's an expert in the field. We can take him to the museum and have him assess the contents. Hopefully he'll have a solution to our dilemma. What do you think?" Riley looked at her fellow detectives.

"Perfect! He's usually in and out of the office throughout the day. Fingers crossed he's in when we get back from class. If not, we can make an appointment," Grant said.

"I just have a weird feeling that something's going to happen soon. Tomorrow, we activate phase one of our plan," Riley declared.

Chapter Eighteen

Many Moving Parts

Later that evening, while the residents of St. Andrews slept, the driver of an old gray truck motored to the Heritage Museum, parked in the back, unlocked the door, and crept inside. He went directly to where the crate of antiquities was stashed. Retrieving it from behind the shelves, he proceeded to leave the building undetected.

Back at the university, he labeled the box for post office pickup and placed it back in the truck with several other packages that were ready to be mailed. His intermediary would be picking up the parcel the day after tomorrow from the designated post office box, delivering the contents to the museum, and collecting the check.

As planned, the foursome met the following afternoon in the science lab hoping to share their information with Professor Abernathy. To their disappointment, the room was empty. Just as they were about to leave, the professor came bustling in through the back door. From the shocked expression on his face, it was obvious that he was startled by the appearance of the teens who had congregated in the lab.

"Did we have an appointment?" Abernathy inquired, quickly thumbing through his calendar.

"No, sir. We're sorry to have barged in on you like this unannounced. You see, we've uncovered some disturbing evidence that we think could point to something illegal. We were hoping that you could advise us on how to proceed," Grant requested.

"Tell me about this evidence that is so disturbing," Abernathy probed.

"If you have the time, sir, it would be easier to show you what we found. Then you can judge if our suspicions are correct," Riley suggested. "It's not that far. The relics we found are in a box at the Heritage Museum in an outer building."

"Looks like you're in luck. My schedule is free for the remainder of the afternoon. Lead the way. I'm anxious to see what mystery the four of you have uncovered," said the professor. He turned off the lights and followed them out the door. As they were exiting the building, Riley caught a glimpse of Colin pulling away in the gray pickup truck.

Hmm, wonder where he's off to and what he has in the truck? Riley pondered.

It wasn't long before the five entered the museum. Professor Abernathy spoke to the curator, letting him know that they would be in the building off the gardens in search of a misplaced carton of antiquities. The request seemed odd to the gentleman, but being that Abernathy was a respected member of the university, he granted the request.

Upon entering the building, Riley and Charlie rushed over to the shelf and began quickly unloading boxes. The excitement in the room was palpable. Once the shelving was clear, Charlie pulled it away from the wall, revealing the small hidden door. Riley yanked the door open. To her dismay, the cavity was empty. She turned to face the others, not knowing what to say.

"It's empty. Someone's moved the box again. See, I told you that something was going to happen soon!" Riley cried, clearly frustrated by this devastating turn of events.

"Now, now, Riley, I'm sure there's a rational explanation for what you think is a nefarious criminal act," Professor Abernathy said soothingly. "I can't imagine anyone affiliated with the museum or university participating in anything illegal. Maybe what you assumed was an act of deception was really a procedure implemented to keep the artifacts safe until they were logged in and catalogued." He gave Riley a gentle pat on her arm. "Now if you'll excuse me, I'll be heading back to my office to wrap up some paperwork. My suggestion? Quit chasing villains. Enjoy the remainder of your stay. Go out and have some fun." And with that bit of advice, Abernathy was out the door. The four disappointed teens reshelved the boxes and departed from the building, not sure what to make of what just had taken place.

"I don't know, maybe he's right," Charlie offered. "Is it possible that we blew this whole scenario out of proportion? I mean, we really don't know the entire process for the delivery and storage of priceless relics."

"Yes, but wouldn't you think if these artifacts are so priceless that they'd be locked up in a safe until they're ready to be authenticated and displayed?" Kenzie questioned.

"Good point, Sis. But where do we go from here?" Grant said. "It looks like we've hit a dead end. So, now we have no relics and no amulet. Thank goodness we chose a career in archaeology and not criminology. I can see it now, Grant and Kenzie detectives extraordinaire, or for a more accurate description, starving artists." He glanced over at Riley and gave her a wink, causing her teenage heart to skip a beat.

"Speaking of the amulet, I've had this nagging thought in the back of my mind. It's like I've seen something that looks familiar, but it won't come together. I think it has something to do with the map," Riley shared, pulling the folded piece of paper from her jeans pocket. The four gathered around the picture to see if one of them might have an epiphany. They scrutinized the photo. It was agreed that the numbers represented feet or yards. It was also obvious that there was a picture of a chipped rock.

"What do you think that rectangle could represent?" Kenzie asked, holding the map at arm's length, then moving it in closer to get a better look. "Well, that didn't clarify anything. It just looks like a rectangle next to a chipped—"

"Wait a minute! I have it," Riley cried. "It's the countermine. Look, the numbers detail how many feet or yards one would walk into the mine. The rock is self-explanatory. But look at the rectangle. Don't you think it could be a light? Remember when I cut my hand on that sharp rock, the rock with a chip, and we held my hand up to the light to assess the damage? It all makes sense. I bet the amulet is buried behind the chipped stone."

"Brilliant, Coz. I do believe you're on to something," Charlie praised. "Let's go!" He was champing at the bit to confirm his cousin's theory.

"I'm anxious to head out right now, but it's getting late. Mom will be expecting us home for dinner. She has also strongly suggested that we begin getting our clothes together, ready to be packed. You know my mom: she's very organized. She would prefer our last night on our vacation to be tranquil. I recommend that we wait until tomorrow. We don't want to raise suspicion, so, guys, let's head out after your class in the afternoon.

"Oh my gosh! I was just thinking, if we don't find the amulet, the two jewels in our possession will have to be turned over to the authorities. If we're bound up in a lot of red tape, it could possibly delay our flight. And if that happens, my parents aren't going to be happy. Fingers crossed that we find the treasure and that it's returned to its rightful place of honor." Riley sighed.

Chapter Nineteen

The Curse

Early the following morning, Ms. Macpherson contacted Barclay, a call that she'd been dreading, confirming that the acquisition was in the works for later that afternoon.

"Take a breath, Barbara. Every detail is in place. If it's any consolation, this is the final arrangement involving you and this intermediary. After this transaction, your job here is complete. I'll be out of the building like we discussed. We don't want to raise any eyebrows and sabotage the deal. There've been too many prying eyes around here as of late. After you're in possession of the artifacts and the check has been cut, you know what to do. I have complete confidence in your ability to accomplish our objective," Barclay reassured his accomplice.

While Barclay was spending time trying to reassure Barbara Macpherson, Riley and Charlie were busy helping

Mom get the cottage in order. A thorough cleaning was under way, which took the better portion of the morning.

"Wow! I'm impressed," Mom remarked after seeing what the cousins had accomplished. You two are sure full of pep and vigor today. It's as if someone plugged you in to a hot socket. I can almost feel the electricity emanating from the both of you." She shook her head.

Little does Mom know that we're about to jump out of our skins, Riley thought as she put the broom back in the closet and checked the clock. "Is there anything else you need us to do, Mom? We're supposed to meet the twins in about fifteen minutes." She was hoping that her mom wouldn't come up with another chore.

"Nope. You're good to go. Thanks for all your help. Enjoy your time with Grant and Kenzie. And remember, be careful."

Charlie and Riley tried to act nonchalant as they departed the house. Partway down the street, their casual walk became what some would call a gait, a cross between a speed walk and run. Grant and Kenzie must have been plugged into the same high-voltage socket as they bolted from the science building and rushed to meet the cousins.

"Who's ready to find treasure?" Charlie asked, taking Kenzie's hand and leading the way.

"He's not too hyped." Riley laughed as Grant took her hand, picking up the pace to catch up with his sister and Charlie. "We should be safe. No one knows that we we're coming to the mine or for what reason," Riley concluded as they approached the entrance.

"Yeah, and we didn't mention it to anyone. In fact, Colin was the only person in near proximity when Kenzie asked if I had the map to the mine. I'm sure that he didn't hear anything. He was preoccupied with some paperwork," Grant added.

"Let's see where these numbers take us. It seems that we were quite a ways into the countermine before I slipped and cut my hand," Riley reasoned. "So, I'm thinking that the numbers represent yards, not feet." Riley's assumption proved correct. "There's no light here, so there's no reason to search for a chipped rock."

"Onward, Macduff," Charlie announced in his best Shakespearean voice. The foursome moved forward, watching their footing, careful to prevent a redo of their last experience. They were a few feet short of their calculations when they saw a light up ahead.

"OK, here's the light. Now where is the chipped rock?" Riley questioned, running her hand across the rocks just above her head.

"Wait, I'll turn on my phone light," Grant volunteered. He reached in his back pocket, but his phone was missing. "Great! I can't believe that it fell out of my pocket. Oh, wait. I remember setting it down on the stool when I was unpacking our gear. I'll stop and get it after we find the amulet."

"That's what I like, a positive attitude, a glass-half-full kind of guy," joked Riley. "Hey, Charlie, can you shine some light up where my hand is located?" The tiny light bounced over the stones until it came to a rock slightly alongside Charlie's cousin's hand.

"Yep, this is where you gashed your hand," Grant said, stepping closer to get a better look at the bloodstained wall. The light from Charlie's phone also revealed deep chisel marks around the stone, indicating the rock had possibly been removed and then replaced.

"Ah, guys, how are we going to pry the stone from the wall?" Charlie asked, feeling stupid that they had overlooked something that important.

"Never fear, my fellow detectives, I have in my bag of tricks just the tool required for this delicate excavation," Kenzie said,stepping forward with a small tool resembling a miniature crowbar. She handed the lever over to her friend.

A potpourri of emotions gripped the four as Riley wiggled the tool back and forth. Were they about to make the discovery of a lifetime, or would they experience disappointment once again? The rock was finally dislodged. Charlie moved forward until the light found its way into the cavity. An indistinguishable object was crammed inside. Riley reached in and removed the object from the hollow chamber. Even in the semidarkness, the thistle amulet was breathtaking. Although the faceted gems were dusted over with particles of dirt, the exquisite cut of the stones managed to capture the light, sending fragments of amethyst and emerald-green, in every direction.

"Just imagine, we're holding a piece of history in our hands!" cried Riley. They were so excited that they never heard the approaching footsteps until it was too late.

"What are the four of you doing?" Barclay demanded. "You're destroying property. You could be arrested for defacing a historical site." His voice was raging with anger. "And you, Grant and Kenzie, being students of archaeology, you should know the importance of chronicling and protecting history. I've had my eyes on the four of you for a while now. It seems that you always have your heads together, poking around where you don't belong. So, let's see this piece of the countermine you carelessly chipped off for a souvenir." He walked toward Riley with a menacing expressing distorting his face.

"Stop right there!" Charlie ordered, stepping between his cousin and the threatening madman. "First of all, how did you know that we'd be here? Are you following us? Are you the one who bugged our cottage and threatened our lives?"

"I have no idea what you're talking about. Yes, I followed you here—to deliver your phone. You left it in the lab. Colin came across the phone when he was straightening up the workroom. He overheard you saying that you were going to the countermine. I just happened to be headed in that direction, so Colin asked me if I could track you down and return your cell. But what's this about someone bugging your home and threatening you? Did you tell your parents, and did they notify the authorities?" He was seemingly shocked at what he had just heard. "It's possible that with all your snooping, you unknowingly put yourselves in harm's way," Barclay concluded.

"No, we didn't share any information with my parents or the police," Riley countered. "The four of us agreed that we didn't have enough evidence to take to the police. Our theory is that someone was either playing a prank or knew we had discovered clues that would lead us to the amulet and wanted to scare us away."

"Well, that still doesn't explain why you're vandalizing a famous landmark," Barclay said, reprimanding the four teens.

"No, sir, you're mistaken," Charlie said. "We've found the royal thistle amulet. Show him, Riley." Charlie stepped back so Barclay could see the treasure in Riley's hand. Before Barclay could respond, another body emerged from the shadows.

"My, my, my, so what do we have here?" Professor Abernathy inquired of the small party gathered in the narrow tunnel.

"Thank goodness you're here!" Kenzie cried. "I think that we've really upset Barclay. We tried to explain that we're not here to deface property You see, we found the thistle amulet. So, now it can be returned to the museum in Edinburgh!"

"Well, good for you. You must be very proud of yourselves. See, things always work out for the best. I know that you were extremely disappointed when the artifacts went missing from the box and you couldn't stop someone from benefiting from participating in something illegal, but this discovery is so much more significant!" Abernathy praised.

"Speaking of nefarious acts," Barclay said, interrupting, "Professor Abernathy, I think it's time that I let you in on the undercover sting going down at the museum as we speak. This setup has been in the works for months. The intermediary closing on the artifact transaction this afternoon should be in handcuffs by now. So, it's a great day all around. I'm quite sure that when the authorities offer the guy a plea deal, he'll be happy to give up the name of his collector. By the way, Riley, what was in the box that Professor Abernathy was referencing?" Barclay was intrigued by this new revelation.

"We took a picture of the items, then researched them. We found grooved-ware pottery. I think there were two polished stones and—"

"A towie ball?" Barclay asked, interrupting. "Well, I must admit, you are quite the accomplished detectives. Those are part of the artifacts included in today's illegal transactions. I really should be angry with the four of you for snooping around and poking your noses in where they don't belong. Ms. Macpherson and I were afraid that you were going to derail the entire maneuver. But no harm, no foul. And I guess I owe the four of you an apology for accusing you of vandalism." Barclay's tone was apologetic.

It was at that precise moment when everyone's guard was down that Professor Abernathy struck Barclay from behind with the butt of his gun that he had hidden behind his back. Barclay let out a cry and fell to the ground. The four teens were dumbstruck. It took a few moments to process what had just happened. Holding the gun on the terrified group, Abernathy stepped over Barclay's body and snatched the amulet from Riley.

"Why couldn't you have left well enough alone?!" he snapped. "I was so close to amassing a substantial fortune. Money I could have used to continue my research. Money I was denied because, in the opinion of the university, I was no longer relevant. I hadn't published in years. They were ready to just toss me aside." His voice became increasingly shrill with every word.

"So, it was you? You were the person behind the threatening notes?" Riley asked, fighting to stay calm. "Were you also responsible for the incident involving the excursion to the island and me being locked in the storage room?" Her hands were balled into tight fists at her side.

"At this stage of the game, what difference does it make? You're all still alive and unharmed. Well, that is, if you behave yourselves. It's obvious that my arrangement with the museum is no longer viable. But thanks to you, I have this valuable little trinket." He snickered, looking down at the priceless amulet lying in the palm of his hand.

"Oh, and poor Barclay. He's going to be extremely disappointed when he regains consciousness and learns that the authorities will have quite a difficult time trying to tie me to the sale of the artifacts. There are several people interceding on my behalf. By the time they proceed up the chain of collectors to me, I'll be out of the country and on my way to becoming a very rich man," Abernathy jeered. With the treasure clenched tightly in one hand and the gun poised to fire in the other, he began backing out of the mine.

But as fate would have it, as Abernathy was stepping over Barclay's body, he slipped on the wet stone floor. His awkward position made it impossible for him to catch his balance. As he fell backward, his head slammed into the unforgiving rock wall. The severe blow to his head caused the gun and the amulet to be jarred from his hands, and they fell to the rock floor. Then came silence. Both the professor and Barclay lay lifeless in the narrow cavern. Grant was the first to react.

"Charlie, hand me your phone. I'll dial the authorities," Grant ordered. "I'll inform them that we need medical assistance and also the police." After the call, Grant glanced over at Riley. "How are you doing? Even in this dim light, you look a little pale. What do you say that we wait for the police outside?"

"I'm fine. I'm still trying to wrap my head around what just happened," Riley replied as she headed out, carefully stepping over Abernathy's crumpled body.

"What about you, Kenzie? Are you doing OK?" Charlie asked, taking her by the hand and helping her out of the mine.

"All good, Charlie. I'm with Riley. It's like, what just happened? Who would believe that one of the university's most respected archaeologists would turn out to be a criminal? The professor was always so nice and seemed so trustworthy—"

Charlie interrupted. "Yeah, so trustworthy that we shared our concern over the artifacts with him, only to find out now that he was the one behind moving them from place to place. He must have had a good laugh when we revealed the hidden compartment and it was empty." He was unable to hide the resentment in his voice.

The police and ambulance arrived within minutes of the call. Grant and the others met the men outside the entrance to the mine.

"Barclay and Professor Abernathy are in there. The professor is the person behind the illegal sale of the artifacts. He held us at gunpoint. It was lucky for us that as he was stepping over Barclay, he slipped and hit his head."

The medical team worked on Abernathy after he was safely secured in handcuffs. One of the other medics checked on Barclay, who had just regained consciousness. It was recommended that he be examined at the hospital to rule out any signs of a concussion. The medical team who examined the professor determined he suffered a depressed skull fracture, likely occurring from hitting his head on the pointy protruding rock. They explained to the officer in charge that Professor Abernathy couldn't be questioned for several days and, depending on the severity of his fracture, he might need to be placed in a medically induced coma. His fracture may require surgery, and it may take him weeks or even months after the surgery to recover. Abernathy was placed on a stretcher, dragged out of the mine, and carried to the ambulance, where he was whisked away to the local hospital.

"Can anyone else see the irony in what just occurred?" Riley asked, looking at each face to see if they had made the connection. "You know what they say about karma. Lars stole the amulet and ended up fracturing his skull, causing him to fall to his death. And now we have almost the same scenario. Professor Abernathy also took possession of the amulet to enrich himself, and he met with a similar fate. To those well-intentioned, the amulet is a blessing. To those with dishonorable, self-serving intentions, the amulet is a curse."

Before anyone could confirm Riley's theory, the police came over and took possession of the amulet and the gun, requesting that the four teens go with them to the police station to give their statements.

"We'd better call my parents so they can meet us down at police headquarters," Riley suggested apprehensively. "I suspect that this surprise is not going to go over very well."

Chapter Twenty

Truth and Consequences

Riley made the dreaded call to her parents. She remembered to tell her mother about the two priceless gems that had been stashed away for safekeeping, asking her to bring them when she came to police headquarters.

When Riley's parents arrived, they were escorted into a private room where the four teens were waiting to give their statements. Mom had contacted the twins' parents to inform them of the current situation. After hanging up, the McGregors had contacted the police chief, announcing they would be arriving within the hour. Riley jumped up from her seat and walked over to her parents when they entered the room, giving them both a hug.

"OK, young lady, why have your father and I been summoned to police headquarters?" Mom asked in total disbelief that they had found themselves in this inconceivable situation.

"I'm so sorry, Mom and Dad. This has turned out to be a nightmare," Riley whispered, choking back tears. "I know that we gave our word to leave well enough alone. And it's not an excuse, but if we would have just stuck to finding the amulet, I don't think any of the dangerous events would have occurred. We kind of fell into discovering the illegal artifacts by accident, and at that point we didn't know what to do." Her voice trailed off as she didn't know what else to say. Charlie left his seat and went over to address his aunt and uncle.

"I apologize too, Aunt Eleanor and Uncle Donald. We certainly didn't mean to ruin this awesome vacation. The four of us got caught up in this mystery and it snowballed, taking on a life of its own," Charlie explained sheepishly. "I have a strong suspicion that our detective days have come an end. And, my dear cousin"—he turned to face Riley—"as I gaze into my crystal ball, I can see that all your *Nancy Drew* books have been confiscated and packed away." He was hoping against hope that his comments would lighten the mood. Judging by the expression on his aunt and uncle's faces, his ill attempt at humor had missed the mark.

Kenzie and Grant were about to speak when their parents were escorted into the room. Looking right past the twins, Mr. McGregor turned his attention to the chief.

"Good afternoon, Chief. I'm Roy McGregor, and this is my wife, Colleen. We're Grant and Kenzie's parents. Are my children being charged with something?" he asked, his face wearing the same look of bewilderment as Riley's parents'.

"Nice to meet you. And to answer your question, no, I just have a few questions about what the four teens witnessed in the mine, and then they're free to leave," the chief stated, signaling for the four to be seated.

"Dad, Kenzie and I are so sorry. We can only imagine how disappointed you and Mom must be," Grant said, his face turning beet red, obviously embarrassed by the unfortunate set of circumstances that had led to this meeting.

"We'll discuss this later," Grant's dad responded brusquely. "We don't want to waste the officer's time. Please go ahead with your questions." He gave the chief a nod.

The chief of police relayed the sequence of events that had led to the arrest of Professor Abernathy. Riley's parents listened intently, horrified with the knowledge that these four teenagers could have been seriously injured. The police chief couldn't help but notice the look of angst on the faces of Riley's parents.

"In hindsight, we all realize the gravity of the situation," remarked the chief. "I'm positive that had these four teens known that their discovery could escalate into their being held at gunpoint, they would have chosen a different course of action. What I do know for certain is that their quest to uncover the stolen amulet eventually led to the detainment and arrest of Professor Abernathy. As you both heard in their statements, the professor was well on his way to escaping with the amulet and avoiding prosecution for selling artifacts owned by the Crown." Even after these positive remarks, Riley's parents' body language signaled that the four squirming teens were not out of the woods.

"OK, folks, I detect there's an underlying issue that needs to be addressed between parents and kids. I have all your contact information if I need to get in touch with you after you get back to the States. So, I think that we're done here. Have a safe flight. And to the amateur detectives seated before me, I thank you for your service on behalf of the Crown," he concluded, shaking hands with the teens.

The silence was deafening on the ride home. Grant and Kenzie were dropped off at their dorm. A short time later, Riley and Charlie were sitting in the living room waiting for the hammer to fall. Both parents acknowledged the positive outcome of the events that had unfolded. That conversation was brief. The two cousins sat and listened as Mom expressed her disappointment with their behavior.

"I'm going to tell you what my mother once told me about not telling the truth. You see, once you lie to someone, you lose that person's trust. And once that trust is lost, it's hard to regain. After having that discussion with my mom, I knew that I would never want to jeopardize that bond between us," she concluded.

"I get it, Mom. Charlie and I were intentionally being untruthful. We were only thinking about solving the mystery of the stolen amulet, even though you asked us not to get involved. We deserve whatever punishment you and Aunt Jan hand out," Riley responded, ashamed of her and Charlie's deceitful actions.

"Well, I'm happy that you admit that your conduct was unacceptable," Dad admonished. "The consensus among the four parents is that you're both grounded for the remainder of the summer. And no cell phones for two weeks."

"I think that's fair," Charlie admitted, looking crestfallen.

"I realize that we'll have to earn back your trust. It's funny, you don't understand the importance of trust until you lose it." Riley choked as tears began streaming down her face.

Riley and Charlie were allowed to meet with the twins the following day to say their goodbyes. Grant's and Kenzie's punishments echoed those meted out by the other adults. Hugs and pats on the back were exchanged, along with promises to keep in touch. On a brighter note, the twins were due to visit their aunt and uncle next summer.

"If we're all well-behaved, maybe we can get together at our house," Riley suggested hopefully. "*Bree-Z* is waiting."

"You might want to reconsider that offer," Charlie warned, flailing his arms as if he were drowning.

"Real funny, Charlie," Riley retorted, giving her cousin a punch in the arm. Last goodbyes were shared.

Charlie and Riley sat together on the plane ride home, each reflecting on their trip to St. Andrews and sharing the highlights. For a while, Riley was lost deep in thought, seemingly grappling with some profound realization.

"OK, Coz, I can tell by the weird look on your face that you're doing that cow ruminating thing. What's up?" Charlie asked, turning toward Riley.

"I was just thinking about the amulet. You know how I said earlier that it could be a blessing or a curse? Well, to Lars and Professor Abernathy, it was a curse. To the Scottish soldiers, it was a blessing. And then there's us. Although we lied over and over to our parents, we had the best of intentions, found the amulet, and then proceeded to get grounded, which in my mind is kind of like being cursed. Although it did seem to protect us from harm. So, I'm wondering if the Scottish thistle has a moral compass. We weren't injured, but we did receive a punishment," she concluded pensively.

"I guess we'll never know," Charlie responded, shrugging his shoulders, leaning back in his seat, and closing his eyes.

Epilogue

Riley and Charlie spent the last few weeks of their vacation grounded. The minute Riley was given permission to use her phone, she called her cousin.

"This has been the worst last weeks of summer vacation ever!" she cried. "All I've been doing is reading, watching seagulls dive for their dinner, watching freighters chugging up and down the river, and watching ducks and swans gliding through the water in search of some small seaweed morsel. Yep, that pretty much sums up the spellbinding entertainment every day on the beautiful Saint Clair River. I can't wait for school to begin!" Riley complained.

"I hear you, Coz. My daily routine sounds as exciting as yours." Charlie yawned. "Bet you're not reading any mystery novels. I guess for the time being, you should probably keep those detective juices of yours in check." He laughed.

"You won't get any argument from me. Our last escapade caused me to do some real soul-searching. Not only did we lie to my parents, but also we allowed our quest for the amulet to put all of us in danger. The worst part is that I disappointed my parents. The punishment was fair, but I've been grounded for so long that I think that I've started to take root." Riley sighed.

* * *

The summer finally came to an end. The cousins embraced their daily routines. Both teens were active in extracurricular activities, and before long, fall was pushing summer out of the way.

One lovely brisk fall afternoon, Riley arrived home to find Mom and Dad discussing a certified envelope that had been hand-delivered.

"Hi, Mom and Dad. What do you have there that's so interesting?" Riley asked, moving closer to get a peek.

"It's a royal invitation to a ceremony being held at the museum in Edinburgh commemorating the return of the Scottish thistle amulet," explained Dad. "Our presence, as well as that of Charlie's parents and the twins and their parents, is requested. The royal family is paying for all our airfare and accommodations while we're in Scotland. The ceremony will take place during winter break, so you won't miss school. So, it looks like Scotland will be getting another dose of the Boyle family. Although this time the dose won't be as hard to swallow, right?" Dad's expression indicated that there would be no more nonsense.

* * *

It seemed like forever before winter break finally arrived. Early that frosty morning, the families boarded the plane. Riley and Charlie sat together. Much of their discussion centered on the ceremony and what exactly their roles would be in the commemoration. As the plane began its descent, the conversation turned to the twins and how great it would be to see them again in person. Communicating online served a purpose, but it was nothing compared to being together face-to-face.

A car was waiting for the families when they landed, and it whisked them off to a lavish hotel. The twins and their parents greeted everyone when they arrived. After settling in, the group of ten met at a nearby restaurant for dinner. Grant and Kenzie filled the Boyle family in on Professor Abernathy and the latest changes at the university.

"Professor Abernathy had surgery and a long rehab and is now serving time in prison. Colin was promoted to Professor Abernathy's position, and from what I hear, he is doing an excellent job," Grant shared.

"My turn," Kenzie jumped in, interrupting her brother. "Barclay has been appointed curator to the St. Andrews Museum and is continuing his research on expediting dig sites. Ms. Macpherson has returned to the Edinburgh Museum as curator. We'll be seeing her tomorrow." Once Kenzie finished, she caught her breath.

After dinner, the four teens chose to walk back to the hotel instead of riding with their parents so that they could have some alone time. Grant and Riley led the way hand and hand, with Kenzie and Charlie bringing up the rear. Each teen shared their prediction about what they thought would happen tomorrow at the commemoration. It was a short walk. And for the two couples, it ended far too soon. Good-nights were exchanged, and then it was off to bed. Tomorrow was a big day, and they had no idea what to expect.

The sky was overcast on the morning the families departed for the museum. Everyone's spirits were high—quite the contrast from their previous visit. Ms. Macpherson met the visitors at the entrance and escorted them to the exhibit. The group gathered around the display, eager to see the amulet showcased in all its grandeur. They weren't disappointed.

The rich, sparkling, multifaceted deep-purple amethyst gemstones, representing the thistle, and the vibrant emerald-green gemstone stem encased in a delicate filigree silver setting was an exquisite artistic rendering of one of the country's national treasures. The party was captivated by its flawless beauty.

"Wow! She sure cleaned up nice after being buried for almost a hundred years." Charlie laughed.

"The intricacy of the design is magnificent," Mom remarked, turning her attention back to the curator.

"It's so nice to see you again, Ms. Macpherson. You're looking lovely. After all the drama last year, I hope that your life is back to normal," Mom said sympathetically.

"Thank you for your concern, Mrs. Boyle. I'm doing fine. There are no more covert stings in my future. Being curator of this magnificent museum is excitement enough for this woman. I must let you all in on a little secret. When I first met Riley and Charlie and overheard their conversation about the amulet, I had a quirky thought that they just might be the duo to unearth clues that the police had overlooked and eventually locate the stolen amulet. And, lucky for us, they were persistent. Although it did get a bit dicey there for a while," Macpherson said, her voice trailing off as a member of the Royal Guard marched in. "We're ready to begin."

The guard stepped up to the exhibit.

"As I announce your name, will you please step forward? Miss Riley Boyle. Mr. Charlie Boyle. Miss Kenzie McGregor. Mr. Grant McGregor. A letter from His Majesty the King of Scots."

The guard read, "'While I may not be able to attend this joyful event in person, I'd like to express my heartfelt thanks for the courage and integrity you exhibited in the discovery and return of the Scottish thistle amulet, one of Scotland's national treasures. As you know, this thistle talisman is a reminder of Scotland's independence, pride, bravery, and perseverance. Some also believe that the thistle has mystical properties. Thank you, sincerely, for the part you all played in returning this antiquity to its distinguished place of honor. Signed, the King of Scots.'"

The guard continued, "Before this ceremony concludes, I have orders to present each of you with a royal envelope. In this envelope you'll find a small token of appreciation. His Majesty requests that the envelopes be opened in my presence."

At the precise moment the teens were about to discover what gift the envelope concealed, the sun broke through the clouds, sending forth dazzling rays of light through the skylight. No one was prepared for what happened next. The minute the sun's rays struck the amulet, there was a flash. The gems seemed to explode. Their brilliance erupted in amethyst and emerald-green fractured sparks. The shimmering colors ricocheted off the ceiling and walls. The fireworks display lasted several seconds, then stopped as abruptly as it had started.

"Speaking of mystical properties, what was that all about?" Charlie asked, trying to make sense of what he had just witnessed.

"Maybe the designer used a triangular or kite-shaped facet," Ms. Macpherson suggested. "These facets spread outward from the center of the gem and give off the most sparkle of any cut. In other words, it reflects and refracts light and therefore increases the gem's luster."

"Well, there sure was a lot of refracting and reflecting going on," Charlie replied, not sounding convinced by the plausible explanation.

"Ahem." The guard interrupted. "I realize that what we have all just experienced is a bit unnerving, but we must return our attention to the matter at hand." He pointed to the envelopes. The parents looked on as the teens each extracted a legal document. The expression on Riley's face was one of pure shock. The others reacted in the same manner.

"What is it?" Dad asked, obviously not expecting the reaction that was now resonating from all four kids. Riley showed her dad the document. Charlie, Grant, and Kenzie handed the paperwork to their parents as well.

"Oh my! This is anything but a *small* token," Mom cried. "This small token will pay for your college tuition for the next four years. I don't know what to say. This is extremely generous."

"No need for words. As you see, there are instructions for the transfer of funds to your respective banks. So, at this time I must take my leave." He closed with a slight bow and a click of his heels.

"Well, I guess that concludes our ceremony," Ms. Macpherson said. "And what a ceremony it was!" She turned to shake hands with the small party. After saying goodbye, Riley, Charlie, Grant, and Kenzie went back to the exhibit for one last look at the priceless antiquity that had brought them together during a summer they would never forget. A feeling of pride and wonderment came over them as they gazed upon the breathtaking antiquity and thought about all that it symbolized.

Later that evening, after dinner, when the four teens were alone, they reflected on the day's events.

"This entire experience has renewed in me a sense of the importance of family, friends, and honesty. It's almost as if the amulet does have mystical properties," Riley theorized.

"What do you mean?" Grant asked, somewhat confused by Riley's statement.

"It just seems that once all of us took responsibility for our behavior and truly regretted what we had done, well, it's like the amulet knew, as if it had some power that could channel good fortune in our direction. I don't know, maybe I'm crazy, but somewhere in my heart I feel that the Scottish thistle amulet truly is a—"

"A blessing!" the four cried in unison.

Printed in the United States
by Baker & Taylor Publisher Services